"What's got into you?" Crispin demanded

Cornered, Tressy burst out, "Well, if you must know, I dislike seeing Nora making a fool of herself over you."

"But maybe I don't think she's making a fool of herself."

Tressy eyed him suspiciously. "You're—you're serious about Nora?" It was impossible to be tactful with this man. "You're all wrong for Nora! She isn't in your league."

"Don't you think that if Nora were my wife, I would want to make her happy?"

"Oh, yes, for a time. But then you'd start to despise her because she would try too hard to please you."

Crispin gave her an odd kind of look. "And if it were you, would you try to please me?"

"No!" Tressy retorted violently.

Books by Sally Wentworth

HARLEQUIN PRESENTS

HARLEQUIN ROMANCE

These books may be available at your local bookseller.

Don't miss any of our special offers. Write to us at the following address for information on our newest releases.

Harlequin Reader Service
P.O. Box 52040, Phoenix, AZ 85072-2040
Canadian address: P.O. Box 2800, Postal Station A,
5170 Yonge St., Willowdale, Ont. M2N 6J3

SALLY WENTWORTH

the wings of love

Harlequin Books

TORONTO • NEW YORK • LONDON
AMSTERDAM • PARIS • SYDNEY • HAMBURG
STOCKHOLM • ATHENS • TOKYO • MILAN

Harlequin Presents first edition August 1985
ISBN 0-373-10814-1

Original hardcover edition published in 1985
by Mills & Boon Limited

CHAPTER ONE

'But I don't want to go. Why should I?' Tressy Sinclair slammed her coffee mug on the kitchen table and stood up, her anger too strong to be contained.

Her mother looked at her unhappily and, with a sigh, began to plead. 'It's only for three months or so. Most girls would jump at the chance of spending the summer on the French Riviera; I know I would.'

'Then you go,' Tressy answered rudely, then shook her head, impatient with herself for having made such a silly remark. 'All right, you don't have to say it; I know they want me and not you. Although why they couldn't have asked you as well I don't know—they can certainly afford it.'

'Your uncle says in his letter,' Mrs Sinclair pointed out patiently, 'that they want you to go along as a sort of companion for Leonora. It'll be like a holiday. And you could do with one, love. You've worked hard enough these last few years.'

'Rubbish!' Tressy answered scornfully. 'They weren't interested in me before I got my qualification as a beautician and hairdresser. They just want me along as some kind of glorified lady's maid to Aunt Grace and Nora.'

'Leonora,' her mother corrected tiredly.

'It was always Nora before they got ambitions to climb the social ladder.'

'But you can't say they ignored you, Tressy. You spent lots of holidays with them when you were a child.'

'Yes—always as the poor relation, always pointed

out to their friends as the object of their munificence. Until I refused to show abject gratitude all the time; they soon stopped asking me then.' Putting her hands on the back of a chair, she leaned forward earnestly. 'And it would be just the same this time, Mum. I'd hate every minute of it. And I'm sure they just want to use me.'

'But your uncle did help pay for you to go to college, Tressy. You owe him for that.'

'But I swore I'd pay him back every penny, and I intend to. Every time I get a commission I put a percentage into the Post Office. But I've hardly got started yet—you know that.'

'Yes, of course I do.' Mrs Sinclair looked at her daughter with sympathy, knowing just how hard she'd worked, first at college, then at trying to establish her own freelance business, visiting clients in their homes to give them a complete beauty treatment, usually before they attended some special function, in the meantime supplementing her income by taking whatever temporary jobs she could get, mostly modelling or demonstrating.

'And I'm just starting to get known,' Tressy added urgently. 'People I've worked for are recommending me to their friends. If I go away for three months now that will be lost and I'll have to start all over again when I get back. You can't ask me to do it, Mum. It just isn't fair!'

'*I'm* not asking you to do it. It's your Uncle Jack. And you've got to admit that he's been good to us. He didn't have to help when your father left us.'

'No, but it was the way he did it—telling you to ask him when you needed anything, so that every time you had to go to him you felt as if you were begging. He could easily have made you an allowance, so that you were at least left with *some* pride, for God's sake!'

Her voice sharp, her mother said, 'You don't have to speak like that about him, Tressy. I was very ill after your father left. If it hadn't been for Uncle Jack you might have been put into a home, and I might have lost you, too.' Abruptly she stood up, and picking up the coffee mugs, stepped to the sink and began to wash them.

Tressy looked at her mother's back, at her hair, prematurely greying because of the years of worry and work. She had no real choice, she knew that. She either had to do what her uncle wanted or else make the complete break and leave home altogether. And although she often didn't see eye to eye with her mother and there were rows, Tressy wasn't prepared to desert her, even though she knew she would probably be happier if she did. Living with a woman whose husband had walked out on her wasn't easy; her mother clung too much. So there was anger and rebellion mixed up with the pity that Tressy felt for her. 'Oh God,' she burst out, 'how I hate being poor!'

Mrs Sinclair turned angrily to face her. 'I've done my best for you, heaven knows.'

'I know, you've told me often enough. But it doesn't stop me from wishing we had some money, does it?'

With an angry glare, her mother said, 'Are you going to accept your uncle's offer or not?' Adding quickly, 'You could look on it as helping to pay him back for what he's done for you.'

'But I didn't want it this way. I wanted to pay him with money, real money that I could have shoved into his fat hands.'

'Yes, well, beggars can't be choosers,' her mother pointed out tartly, her North Country upbringing showing in her speech.

'And so long as you have that attitude you'll never get anywhere,' Tressy retorted. Then, with a resentful sigh, 'Yes, all right, I'll go. *You* give me no choice. And for heaven's sake don't start telling me that I'm sure to have a good time,' she added as her mother smiled and opened her mouth. 'I can think of nothing worse than being stuck with Nora and her parents for three months!'

For a moment they stood and faced each other angrily, then Mrs Sinclair turned and went into the hall where she picked up the phone. Tressy watched her for a moment and then went up to her room. As she climbed the stairs she heard her mother saying, 'Yes, of course, Jack, Tressy would love to come. It's very kind of you to invite her . . .'

Unlike his younger brother, Tressy's father, Jack Sinclair had always done well, inheriting a small building business and turning it into a thriving concern with an annual turnover well into seven figures, as he never tired of telling everyone. He lived, still, in the same town where he had been born, Oldham in Lancashire, an industrial county in the north of England, but now he lived in a very large Edwardian house on the edge of the town instead of in the old cottage next door to the builder's yard. He had sent down some money to pay for Tressy's journey and there was just enough for the train fare and for a taxi to the house. The driver's tip Tressy had to find herself, presumably her uncle either hadn't taken it into account or didn't give them. She supposed, cynically, that she ought to think herself lucky he hadn't expected her to take the bus.

Her aunt and Nora greeted her perfunctorily, too engrossed in packing for the holiday and closing up the house for the summer to take much notice of her. They were to spend one more night in England and then catch a plane from Manchester Airport to Nice early tomorrow morning.

'You can help Leonora to pack,' Aunt Grace instructed her soon after she'd arrived. 'I'm sure we're not going to have enough cases,' she added with an anxious frown. 'Have you got any room in yours?'

'No,' Tressy replied firmly. 'Where's Uncle Jack?'

'He's still at the yard. And I expect he'll stay there until he's good and sure that all the packing's done,' she said bitterly. 'He's left me to see to everything. Just like a man!' She bustled off; she was a very big woman, the complete opposite to her name, and Tressy marvelled at the optimism her parents had shown in giving it to her. But then you never could tell how tiny babies in their cradles were going to turn out.

Tressy went up with Nora to her room and looked with some misgivings at the three large half-filled suitcases that were on the bed. Most of the drawers and wardrobes were open and there were odd piles of clothes on chairs and the floor.

Nora sighed. 'I don't know where to start. Mummy said I've got to get everything packed today, but I can't decide which things to take.' There were fitted wardrobes all along one wall, and going to one, she opened the door and ran her hand along the things inside indecisively, pulling out a couple of dresses. 'I think I'd better take these. Although if I pack them now they'll get awfully creased.' She brightened. 'But that doesn't matter, because Mummy said you could iron them for me when we get there.'

'Oh, did she?' Any willingness Tressy had to help her cousin died stillborn. Picking up a pile of underclothes from a chair, she put them on the floor and sat down, crossing her long legs. 'Are you going to take any pairs of trousers with you? You should really put those at the bottom of the cases.' Sitting back in her chair, she began to tell the other girl what to do.

Tressy was well experienced in handling Nora, all you had to do was to give her frequent and uncomplicated instructions and she would happily carry them out. It came from having had a convent schooling, although Nora wasn't a Catholic, it had simply been the fashionable school for all the rich men of the area to send their daughters to. There Nora had got used to being told what to do every minute of the day and she still responded to it.

Tressy watched her cousin while she packed, trying to define what was different about her since the last time she and her aunt had stayed with them in London, using her mother's house as a free hotel while they went on a shopping spree. The most noticeable thing was that Nora was much thinner; a true offspring of her mother, Nora was meant to be a big girl, she was tall, about five feet nine inches, the same as Tressy, but where Tressy was slender with a delicate bone structure, Nora was big-boned and usually on the plump side. But now she must have lost quite a lot of weight, but it didn't suit her, she just looked gaunt.

'Have you been ill?' Tressy asked her.

'No. Oh, you've noticed that I'm slimmer,' said Nora with satisfaction. 'I've been on a crash diet, at a health farm.'

Personally Tressy thought she looked far from healthy, but there had been a trace of smugness in Nora's voice, as if she was keeping something to herself. Looking at her cousin more carefully, Tressy noticed, too, that she'd had her hair done in a far more sophisticated style and, if Tressy was any judge, she'd also had the colour lightened to make it fairer. They were both twenty-one, Tressy being the elder by six months, but their different environments had made them develop at different rates so that Tressy had always felt light years older than Nora, but now she wondered if her cousin was starting to catch up at last and assert her own personality. And there was an intriguing hint of excitement in her manner, too. Tressy decided to find out the reason for it.

Getting up, she went and knelt by one of the many large boxes on the floor with a very famous name on the lid and opened it. 'What have you got in here?'

She began to unwrap the layers of tissue paper, but Nora rushed over and snatched the box from her. 'Don't touch that—it's my new underwear.'

'Really? Why can't I look at it? Do show me, Nora.'

'No, they're private.'

But it didn't take more than a few minutes of mixed persuasion and bullying for Nora to eventually join her on the floor and take the things out of the box one by one. Tressy caught her breath, entranced by the delicate silk garments in palest pink, edged by the finest lace, real lace. Nora had the whole set: full slip, bra, suspender belt, French knickers, tiny bikini pants, camisole and nightdress; the whole works.

'My God, Nora, they're beautiful!' Tressy put out a reverent fingertip to gently touch the lace. 'They must have cost a small fortune. Were they a present or something?'

'Well, sort of,' Nora owned smugly, carefully putting each garment back into the box. 'Mummy bought them for me, and loads of other things too. I need them, you see, for—for France.'

Tressy glanced at her sharply, noticing the hesitation. 'But you've been to France for holidays before, haven't you?' she asked casually.

'Yes, but this is—well, different.'

'In what way?' Tressy demanded, wondering why she'd been specifically asked along on this year's trip.

'Well,' Nora tried to look coy, but it just didn't

work on her, she just looked silly, 'actually, we'll be seeing someone there that I know.'

'A man?' Tressy hardly needed to guess. 'Why, Nora, you old slyboots! Don't tell me you've fallen in love? Who's the lucky man?' she asked with smiling mockery.

Nora looked at her uncertainly for a moment, but she had never been able to tell when Tressy was taking the mickey out of her and, reassured by her smile, she happily launched into the whole story. 'Oh, he's wonderful, really fabulous! Daddy met him through business and brought him back here for a meal one evening. I fell for him straight away. He's so *masterful*, Tressy, you wouldn't believe. And terribly good-looking. And Mummy and Daddy like him, too.' Her cheeks flushed with excitement as she went on eagerly. 'The next time he came up north Daddy invited him to stay here with us and I really got to know him then.'

'He isn't local, then?'

'No, he lives in London. He's the managing director of a big finance company in London, and terribly well off, Daddy says. He bought Mummy a beautiful crystal vase as a present for having him to stay. And he was only here for two days. Of course he was going to stay longer, but something cropped up and he had to go back early. He was really sorry he had to go; he said so. And he sent Mummy a charming note with the vase. He has perfect manners. And you really feel— feminine when you're with him. D'you know what I mean? He makes you feel like a lady. Always standing up when you come into the room and opening the car door for you and all that.'

Tressy looked at her cousin in fascination as she came to a breathless stop; she didn't think she'd ever heard Nora talk so enthusiastically about anything before, certainly not about a boy, although she'd had the usual schoolgirl crushes in the past. 'He sounds fantastic. But you haven't told me his name or how old he is.'

'His name is Crispin, Crispin Fox. And he's thirty-two.'

'Crispin? What kind of a name is that?' Tressy laughed derisively.

'It's an old family name,' Nora said defensively, adding, 'And anyway, you shouldn't laugh at other people's, with a name like Tressilian.'

Mentally, Tressy once again cursed her parents for bestowing that name on her. 'No, you're right,' she admitted. 'Perhaps he hates his name, too. Do you call him Cris?'

Nora shook her head. 'He isn't the type who has a nickname.'

Tressy looked at her speculatively; even allowing for Nora's natural over-enthusiasm, the man sounded quite a catch. 'You're not engaged to him?'

Nora flushed. 'No, not yet.'

'But you must know him quite well if you've arranged to go on holiday together.'

Again Nora blushed. 'Well, we're not actually going together. He has a motor yacht that he keeps at Monte Carlo, but we're taking a villa at Cap Martin, just outside Monte Carlo.'

'But you've arranged to meet him there?' Tressy persisted when the other girl seemed reluctant to go on.

'Well—er—the fact is . . . Mummy did say that we would be there at the same time as him, and he said he'd look us up and take us all for a trip on his boat,' Nora finished lamely.

Tressy stared at her. 'Just how many times have you met him?'

'I told you: he came to dinner and then he came to stay.'

'And how many times has he taken you out exactly?'

'He took me out to dinner the second night he was staying here,' Nora said defensively. 'To the best restaurant in Manchester.'

'Just you—or did your parents go, too?' Tressy asked shrewdly, her eyes on her cousin's face.

'Well, as a matter of fact . . .'

'It was all of you, wasn't it? And on the basis of that you're following him to the south of France? You and Aunt Grace, and probably Uncle Jack as well, are deliberately setting out to chase him! My God, Nora! That's what all these new clothes are for, isn't it? Well? Isn't it?'

Nora got huffily to her feet. 'So what if it is? Mummy told me I wasn't to tell you about him, but I thought you'd understand. It isn't my fault I haven't seen much of him; he works and lives down in London. I did phone and invite him up when it was my birthday party, but he couldn't make it because he had to go to America on business. So how else am I to see him again unless we take him up on his offer to meet him in France?'

'No way, I suppose,' Tressy admitted, looking up at her. 'You've really fallen for this man, haven't you?'

'So what?'

'So don't look at me like that. I'm on your side. If you've really fallen for this Crispin Fox, and marriage is what you want, then I'll help you all I can.' And Tressy meant it; in some ways she felt sorry for Nora, it couldn't always be fun being the only child of rich and socially ambitious parents. They were always pushing her on to be everything they weren't; to speak without a Lancashire accent, to join all the upmarket clubs and societies, to mix with the right people and never put a foot wrong. The sort of life that would make Tressy rebel within a month. But to Nora's credit, she always tried her best to please her parents and seemed contented enough, but until now, she had always lacked any spark of vitality and had been plain dull. Today, though, she seemed more alive than Tressy had ever known her, and if meeting this Crispin Fox did that for her, then Tressy was all for fostering the romance. And it also gave her a lever in dealing with Uncle Jack.

As his wife had prophesied, he didn't come home until just in time for dinner, when all the packing was more or less done. He, too, was a big man—he'd have to be to dwarf Aunt Grace—and he liked to think that he was the master in his own home, which his wife and daughter let him believe until they wanted something. After dinner he announced that he had a few last-minute letters to catch up on and retired to his study. Aunt Grace frowned at him impatiently but didn't try to stop him; everything was done anyway. Ten minutes later, Tressy followed him there, giving a peremptory rap on the door and then walking straight in. She caught him with his feet up on his desk, a pipe of tobacco just beginning to draw in his mouth and not a letter in sight.

He spluttered a bit when she came in and hastily swung his legs down, but Tressy sat in a chair opposite him and said kindly, 'It's all right, I won't give you away. It's nothing to do with me if you sneak in here to get out of the way.'

The word 'sneak' didn't go down very well. He glared at her. 'What is it you want?'

'I want to know how much money you're going to pay me while I'm working for you,' Tressy told him bluntly, coming straight to the point.

'Working for me? But you're not working for me. We're giving you a holiday.'

'Oh no, you're not. The reason you're taking me along is so that I can keep Nora and Aunt Grace looking like fashion plates: do their hair and make-up and look after their clothes. And if I'm going to work like that then I want paying.'

'You seem to forget, my girl, that I put you through college so that you could get your certificates. It seems to me the least you could do is help your aunt and cousin.'

'You didn't put me through college,' Tressy answered coldly. 'All you did was give my mother handouts when she didn't know which way to turn. Why, I bet you even claim for us as dependent relatives against your income tax.'

Jack Sinclair looked slightly abashed and Tressy knew she had guessed right. But he said hotly, 'You realise we're paying your fare, as well as providing your food and accommodation. *And* you'll have plenty of leisure time. What more do you want?'

'Wages,' retorted Tressy, refusing to be pushed into feeling guilt or embarrassment. 'You'd have to pay a hired maid, so you can pay me.'

He glared at her again, hating to be thwarted by someone he thought of as a slip of a girl, but he was a shrewd enough businessman to know when he'd lost. 'All right, if you're that ungrateful for what we're doing for you, I'll give you ten pounds a week.'

Tressy's eyebrows went up and she sighed. 'Let's be realistic, shall we? I'm a trained beautician and hairdresser. And working on Nora and Aunt Grace isn't going to be easy. I want two hundred pounds a week, in advance.'

'*What?*' He nearly fell off his chair. 'You're mad!'

'Am I? When I go to a client's home to give them a private beauty treatment, I never charge less than forty pounds a time. On those terms I wouldn't give

more than five treatments a week between them to
Nora and Aunt Grace. I bet they want a whole lot
more than that. *And* it doesn't include looking after
their clothes.'

Eyebrows raised, Uncle Jack stared at her. 'You
really charge forty pounds a time?' He was so
surprised that he forgot himself and his Lancashire
accent came through thick and strong. 'By 'eck, lass,
you're in't right business there. That's *real* brass.' But
then he remembered himself and said, 'But don't think
I'm paying you that much, because I'm not, and that's
flat.'

'Oh, but I really think I deserve that much.
Especially,' Tressy emphasised, 'now that Nora's
trying to catch a rich husband. After all, you do want
her to look her best for Crispin Fox, don't you?'

'Women,' he muttered bitterly. 'They can't keep
anything to themselves for two minutes!'

So they bargained, both giving way very gradually
until they reached a figure which was a little more
than Tressy had thought she'd have to accept and a
little less than her uncle thought he'd have to pay, so
they both believed they'd made the best of the deal.

'Weekly in advance, though,' Tressy stipulated.

He nodded. 'But there's one condition to all this,' he
said, his voice changing and becoming serious. 'Nora's
told you about this man she fancies, even though I
told her not to. Well, I want your word that you'll
keep away from him. I don't want you butting in.
Nora's all I've got and I want the best for her. And if
Crispin Fox is what she wants then I'll do my best to
see she gets him.' Clumsily, without wanting to be
disloyal, he went on, 'She's no beauty, our Nora, I
know that. Whereas you . . .' His eyes went over
Tressy's arresting face, long auburn hair and slender
figure. He sighed. 'Well, you know what I mean. I

want your promise that you won't try and queer our
Nora's pitch with this man. That you'll stay out of it.'

For a moment Tressy's feelings softened towards
him; for all his faults Uncle Jack loved his daughter.
But then she remembered how his younger brother,
her own father, had walked out on her and her mother,
and her heart filled with jealous bitterness. She
shrugged. 'I'm not on the lookout for a rich husband,
if that's what you mean. I prefer to get where I'm
going by my own efforts.'

He recognised the gibe all right but could afford to
ignore it. 'I'll want your promise.'

'Very well, then,' Tressy answered coldly. 'You
have it.'

'Good.' He wagged his finger at her. 'And I shall
expect my money's worth, mind.'

She laughed and stood up. 'I'm quite sure Aunt
Grace will make sure you get it!'

She went up to bed shortly afterwards and lay
awake for a while, not looking forward to the next
three months but glad that she had managed to screw
some money out of Uncle Jack, although he would be
more than surprised when, at the end of their holiday,
she gave as much of it as she could back to him in
payment for the money he had given to her mother
while she was at college. She had been lucky to get
that much; he must want her services pretty
desperately. This Crispin Fox must be quite something
to set Nora and Aunt Grace in such a tizzy. It would
be interesting to see what he was like in the flesh, even
if she did have to keep out of his way. And interesting,
too, to see what he felt for her cousin. She sighed as
she turned her head into the pillow; it was about the
only thing there was to look forward to on this whole
long working holiday that seemed to stretch into
infinity.

Uncle Jack had a reputation for being tight with his money, but Tressy had to admit, when she saw the villa he had hired for the summer, that he had spared no expense this time. It was a beautiful place, situated on the rocky promontory of Cap Martin that looked across the wide blue bay to Monaco and the skyscrapers of Monte Carlo. The villa was about a hundred and fifty years old and had originally been built for a princess, exiled from her own cold country, who had led a much more sociable and comfortable life in this temperate climate. Since her time it had passed through several ownerships and had been completely and luxuriously modernised and furnished in the best French taste—which was a little overdone to the more sober English eyes. Outside there was a garden shaded by exotic, unfamiliar trees and shrubs, a swimming pool and flights of steps leading down to the beach at the base of the promontory.

After going over the house from top to bottom and taking a look at the nearness of Monte Carlo, Aunt Grace announced that 'it would do' and proceeded to allot rooms. She and Uncle Jack had the best bedroom overlooking the sea, with Nora next to them; Tressy was given a maid's room at the back of the house because they wanted the other bedrooms for when they 'entertained'. It would have been nice to be able to look out over the Mediterranean, but Tressy didn't much care where she slept; she probably wouldn't spend much time in her room anyway.

Rather to her surprise, she had enjoyed the drive along the Corniche road from Nice airport, seeing new vistas of scenery continually opening up both inland and over the sea. And the weather was lovely; mid-June in England was often unsettled, but here the sky was a clear, cloudless blue, the sun hot enough for her to want to swim and sunbathe straightaway. Her aunt, however, had other ideas.

'All our dresses need ironing to get the creases out, and then we'll both need our hair done before we go to the Casino tonight,' she instructed Tressy. 'Leonora, you'd better go and try to get a couple of hours' sleep; I don't want you looking tired when we go out tonight. Off you go. Tressy can unpack the rest of your things later.'

The two cousins went upstairs together and Nora obediently took off her outer clothes and lay on the bed while Tressy collected her dresses.

'Which one are you going to wear tonight?' she asked.

'I thought I'd wear the new black one. Do you think it's all right?' Nora asked anxiously. 'It's not too dressy, is it?'

Tressy held up the one she indicated; it was a black strapless sheath dress with a huge multicoloured silk bow, like butterflies' wings, at the back. It was a stunning dress and must have cost a stunning price, but even without seeing her in it, Tressy knew that it was all wrong for Nora. 'Is it a special gala night or something at the Casino?' she asked carefully.

'Oh no, it's just an ordinary evening.'

'Then why don't you keep this for something special and wear a different one tonight? Like this.' She held up a pretty blue full-skirted one.

But Nora immediately rejected it. 'Oh no, that's quite old. I want to wear something new. And I want to make an impression.'

Tressy looked at her quickly. 'He's going to be there, then, your boy-friend?'

Her cheeks flushing with pleasure at the term, Nora replied excitedly, 'We hope so. Daddy made enquiries and we know he's here in France. Most people go to

the Casino some time in the evening. And if he isn't
there,' she added naïvely, 'Mummy says we can always
walk down to the harbour and see if he's on his yacht.
So I think I will wear the black dress.'

'Okay, if you say so.' Tressy just hoped she didn't
ruin it when she ironed it. 'What's the name of his
boat?'

'It's called *Chimera*. An odd name, isn't it?'

Tressy agreed, and left her to her nap.

There was a well-equipped laundry room in the
basement where she hung the clothes on padded
hangers and began to go carefully through them. As
she worked, Tressy smiled to herself, thinking that
this Crispin Fox didn't stand much of a chance against
the united front of the Sinclair family. She could
almost have felt sorry for the poor man if she hadn't
wanted him to hurry up and get engaged to Nora so
that, with luck, they would all go back to England the
sooner.

She worked all afternoon and later did the women's
hair in the rather formal and, to Tressy's mind, out-
of-date styles that they wanted and made up their
faces. She was good at her job and with make-up was
able to disguise the gaunt look that over-slimming had
given to Nora's face, but nothing could hide the heavy
bone structure of her shoulders revealed by the black
dress. Still, if that was what she wanted and felt good
in ... Tressy turned to Aunt Grace and did what she
could to hide her triple chin; she was the one who
would have benefited from the health farm, not Nora.

They left at eight, intending to have dinner at a
restaurant before going on to the Casino. Left alone,
Tressy unpacked her own things and then went down
to the kitchen to make herself something to eat. There
was quite a lot of food, bought in in readiness for their
arrival, and Tressy liberally helped herself from a jar

of Beluga caviare and to some pâté de foie gras. Piling
all the most expensive things she could find on to a
tray and carrying it into the huge dining room, she set
herself a solitary place at the head of the long, highly
polished antique table and opened a bottle of wine
from the racks in the wine cellar. She knew next to
nothing about wine, but chose one which had the
oldest date she could find on it plus a couple of
cobwebs. Then she went upstairs, changed into a dress
and did her hair and face, then came down to dine in
solitary state. If she couldn't join 'em, then she was
certainly going to do her best to beat 'em!

But even the novelty of eating in such plush
surroundings can soon wear off when you are entirely
alone, and the lights she could see in the distance drew
Tressy to the terrace where she looked out across the
bay to the brilliantly lit coastline of Monte Carlo,
made doubly bright by the reflection in the softly
undulating sea. The lure of those lights proved too big
a temptation to resist; within twenty minutes Tressy
was on a bus, looking eagerly out as it jolted its slow
way down the Lower Corniche and into Monte Carlo.

The bus deposited her at the foot of the vast floodlit
rock on which stood the Royal Palace, and she
automatically began to climb the long flights of steps
that led up to the top. There were lots of other people
about, tourists mostly, taking a stroll after their
evening meals or still eating at the many little cafés in
the old town on top of the rock. Tressy stood with
everyone else and gazed at the Palace, guarded by
soldiers in uniforms straight out of Ruritania, then
wandered round the souvenir shops for an hour or so
before walking back down into the main town.

The famous Casino was some way off, over the
other side of the harbour, with all the best hotels and
most expensive shops clustered around it. As she

walked towards it, Tressy had to pass several youths or young men, in groups or pairs, prowling round the town looking for girls, and most of them tried to attract her attention, one even coming up to her and taking her arm. But Tressy knew how to take care of herself and shook him off, completely ignoring the others; she wasn't in the mood for being picked up. Opposite the Casino there was a square, and she sat there for some time, watching people going into the Casino and coming and going at the hotel nearby, doormen hurrying to open the doors of opulent Rolls-Royce and Mercedes limousines—they were too big to be just called cars. Tressy wondered if she might see her aunt and uncle and Nora, and laughed to herself at the thought of their faces if she tagged along with them into the Casino. But she must have missed them, because they didn't turn up, and presently she had to leave because a man came over and spoke to her in French, obviously propositioning her. Tressy tossed her head at him, her red hair like flames in the lamplight, and walked back down to the harbour, walking quickly, as if she had somewhere definite to go; from experience she had found that men were far less likely to accost you if you walked purposefully.

But at the harbour she slowed down and strolled along, amazed at the size of the private motor yachts there. Some of them were as big as small ships, and she overheard one big and beautiful boat pointed out as belonging to a famous Greek shipping millionairess. Overawed in spite of herself, Tressy walked along, looking for a boat called *Chimera*. She found it, about a hundred yards further along in the shadow of a clifflike rock on which ran the road from the lower town up to the Casino. All the boats in the harbour were moored Mediterranean style, with their sterns against the quay, most of them having short gangways which could be let up or down, leading from a gap in the stern rail to the quay. The *Chimera* wasn't by any means as big as the larger motor yachts in the harbour, but it was big enough. Its gangway was down and there were lights in all the windows as well as in the big open cockpit in the stern. Not wanting to get too close in case her relations were already on board, Tressy looked round and found a flight of steps cut into the rock leading to the upper road. She climbed them and standing in the deep shadow of a tree, found that she had a perfect view down into the *Chimera*. There was a small group of people in the cockpit sitting around with drinks in their hands, and they looked to be members of what the popular press described as the jet set; all sleekly good-looking and dressed in the casually elegant style that spelt money. As different from Uncle Jack and Aunt Grace as chalk and cheese.

Leaning on the iron railing, Tressy peered down from her vantage point to observe them more closely. There were four people, two men and two women. Somehow she got the impression that the women were French, perhaps from their clothes and the way they wore them. They were women rather than girls; both looked to be in their late twenties, and both had dark hair. Tressy strained to listen to find out if she was right, but there was a radio or something playing in the background and she couldn't hear. One of the men had gone into the cabin, but the other was tall and fair-haired, his features handsome in an aristocratic kind of way. He was slumped in a chair, smoking a cigarette and looking rather bored, despite one of the women's obvious attempts to try and divert him. Could this be Crispin Fox? Tressy wondered.

But just then the music came to an end and she distinctly heard one of the women call out something, adding the name 'Crispin'. A moment later the other man came out of the cabin into the full light of the cockpit. He, too, was tall, about six feet two, but there any similarity with the other man ended. The first impression Tressy got was of contained power, of a lithe, muscular body that was used to action, his shoulders and broad chest constrained by the white dinner jacket, his hands more used to emphasis than offering drinks, his deep voice to giving orders instead of making small-talk. He was good-looking—very— with dark hair and even features, but there was toughness and determination in the set of his jaw and thrusting chin, and arrogance in the way he held his head.

Tressy caught her breath. So this was Crispin Fox! Heavens, no wonder Nora had fallen for him! But then she felt a surge of pity for her cousin. This was the kind of man who could eat a girl like Nora for breakfast. He could break her heart and not even notice that he'd done it!

CHAPTER TWO

THE woman who had called Crispin Fox into the cockpit was gesturing down the quay, and Tressy followed her pointing hand to see her three relations making their way down the quay towards the boat. They walked with Nora in the middle, like two elephants guarding their young, taking up so much space that they completely blocked the way.

'Damnation!' The surprised expletive carried to Tressy's ears quite clearly, but she couldn't understand what the others said when they turned to Crispin Fox to ask why he had made it.

Tressy felt suddenly sick, realising now that the man wasn't interested in her cousin. She had half suspected it from the first, but for Nora's sake had hoped that it hadn't been completely one-sided. But there was nothing at all lover-like in Fox's reaction, there wasn't even pleasure at seeing an acquaintance, only annoyance.

As the three of them came nearer, Tressy drew back into deeper shadow, not wanting them to see her, and afraid of moving out into the light in case they did. She would have liked to go now, unwilling to see or hear more, but she had to stay where she was.

'Why, Crispin!' It was Aunt Grace who spoke first, using her best B.B.C. English accent. 'What a lovely surprise! We had no idea you were here yet. And is this your boat?'

He came across the gangplank to greet them, and to his credit and Tressy's surprise, betrayed none of his earlier annoyance. 'Mrs Sinclair. As you say, what a pleasant surprise. Mr Sinclair—Leonora.' He shook hands with each of them in turn. 'When did you arrive?'

'I told you, you must call me Jack,' her uncle said affably. 'We haven't been here long. Just getting our bearings. That's a beautiful boat.'

'Perhaps you'd like to come aboard and look round?'

Crispin Fox had no alternative but to ask them, but he did it politely enough. Nora had difficulty in negotiating the gangplank in her high heels and tight skirt and had to be helped. Then Tressy saw him introduce the newcomers to his friends and get them a drink. They spoke in English and the music was no longer on, but Tressy deliberately tried not to listen. But she could hear Nora's nervous giggle and the sound made her angry, both at Crispin Fox and at Nora herself for being such a fool. Was she so besotted that she couldn't see that the man was way out of her league? He was hardly in the same world, for heaven's sake! Okay, so Uncle Jack had worked himself up into being a millionaire, but he was still a working-class North-Countryman at heart, whereas every aspect of Crispin Fox, from his arrogant head down to his immaculately polished shoes, screamed a public school, Oxbridge, and that complete self-assurance that only inherited money can give. And his friends, too, were sitting back and looking prepared to be amused, as if the three Sinclairs were an unusual cabaret act put on for their benefit.

Angrily Tressy turned away and, taking the risk of being seen, ran out into the lamplight and up the hill, out of sight of the boat. The roads were heavy with traffic and there were lots of people about, even though it was quite late, many of them sitting at the outdoor cafés drinking, or eating huge bowls of ice-cream. After walking aimlessly for some time, Tressy felt thirsty and sat down at one of the tables and ordered a coffee. She was still angry but trying hard not to be—after all, it was nothing to do with her if her relations wanted to make fools of themselves. From the look of this Crispin Fox, he was quite capable of turning round and telling them to get lost when he couldn't stand their pushiness any longer, and from the way he had reacted when he first saw them, that would be sooner rather than later. Perhaps he would do it politely—Tressy hoped he would—but Aunt Grace could be thick sometimes, and there looked to be a cruel streak in Crispin Fox that wouldn't hesitate to put someone down if he wanted to.

The more she thought of him, the more Tressy disliked him. He must have realised that Nora had fallen for him and he could surely have done something to put her off instead of handing out casual invitations to meet here in France. He was obviously experienced enough to know how to handle women, even someone as gauche as Nora, and could have let her down lightly if he had wanted to. To Tressy's mind he was just another male chauvinist, *and* one of the highest order. Tressy didn't have a lot of time for men at the best of times, feeling that you had to use them before they used you, and this Crispin Fox really got up her nose. She was glad that Uncle Jack had made her promise to keep out of his sight, because the less she saw of him the better.

She had finished her coffee some time ago, and the waiter came up and asked if she wanted anything else. But it was late and time to go. Tressy paid him and walked back the way she had come, not wanting to get lost in the maze of streets. Approaching the harbour, she was careful to keep on the other side of the road until she reached a flight of steps which were safely past *Chimera*. She went down them and walked along the quayside, careful not to look back. A fat man cradling an open bottle of whisky in his arms was coming towards her; he was very drunk, reeling from side to side and singing to himself in between bursts of maudlin speech. Tressy looked at him with distaste and moved to the edge of the quay nearest the wall to pass him, but he saw her and stopped, then staggered over to her.

'*Ah, tu es belle, chérie!*'

She tried to get past him, but the man caught her arm and gave a revolting hiccup right in her face. 'Get away from me, you lout!' He was impossible to shake off, holding her in a grip of drunken strength.

'*Embrasse-moi, ma belle,*' he commanded drunkenly, and pushed her back against the wall, trying to kiss her.

'Let go of me!' Tressy kicked him on the shin and he made an indignant sound of pain, but didn't let go, instead pushing his fat body against hers so that she was squashed between him and the wall. 'Go away, damn you!' She hit him round the face this time.

He gave an angry grunt and raised an arm to cuff her, but just as he did so someone grabbed the arm and pulled him sharply away. But as he was yanked round, the drunk's other arm, holding the whisky bottle, swung round, emptying the contents all down Tressy's front.

'Hey, look out!' She gave a yelp and tried to move out of the way, but the whole lot went over her. 'Oh, no!' She looked up from her soaked and stinking dress and saw her rescuer giving the drunk a good shove back the way he had come. Then he turned round and she groaned again; it was Crispin Fox.

Coming over to her, he asked, 'Are you all right?'

But Tressy interrupted furiously, 'Just look what you've done! I've got whisky all over me!'

'What *I've* done?' His eyebrows flew up in surprise.

'Yes. If you hadn't pulled him round like that the whisky wouldn't have gone over me,' Tressy told him crossly.

'Am I to take it you were with him? I beg your pardon,' he said sarcastically. 'I got the impression that you needed some help.'

'No, of course I wasn't with him. And I'm quite capable of taking care of myself, so don't expect me to start thanking you. Oh God, just look at my dress—it'll be ruined!' It was one of her good dresses that she'd managed to get cheaply after a modelling session for a mail order company, a sleeveless shirtwaister in cream linen.

Crispin Fox looked at her critically. 'Not if you wash it straightaway, surely?'

'And just how am I supposed to wash it?' Tressy demanded. 'By the time I get to the bus and go home it will have dried, and then I'll never get the stain out.'

He frowned and then shrugged. 'In that case, you'd better come with me.' And taking hold of her arm, he turned her and began to walk back down the quay.

'Hey! Just where do you think you're taking me?' Tressy hung back as he led her along.

'Back to my boat. You can wash your dress there and dry it.'

'To your boat?' Tressy had a mental picture of walking up to the *Chimera* with her relatives still sitting on the deck, not to mention his other friends, and she stopped and pulled her arm away. '*Oh, no!*'

Crispin Fox, of course, took her refusal the wrong way. 'You don't have to be afraid,' he informed her sardonically. 'You're quite safe. In the little I've seen of you I already know that you're definitely not my type.'

Tressy's head came up and she glared at him. 'The feeling's mutual!'

'So are you coming to wash your dress, or not?'

She was holding the material of the front of the dress away from her, hoping it wouldn't go through to her underclothes, and she looked down at it unhappily, knowing that she couldn't afford to replace it and might as well throw it away unless she did something quickly. 'If I go with you, I'll miss my bus,' she objected, not knowing what to do for the best.

'So get a taxi,' he pointed out, impatiently.

Tressy's indignation flared. 'I can't afford a taxi. Not everyone in the world's loaded, you know. Oh hell, why couldn't you have minded your own business?'

The exasperation in Crispin Fox's dark eyes turned to anger. 'Very well,' he said coldly. 'As you obviously blame me for the accident to your dress, then I'll pay for your taxi home—or for a replacement dress if you prefer not to accept my offer of help,' he added harshly.

His tone made her look at him quickly and see the dislike in his eyes. No, she certainly had nothing to fear from him. But she was being unfair and she knew it. She bit her lip, thinking of her promise to Uncle Jack. 'Is there anyone else on your boat?' she demanded abruptly.

He took her question the only way he could take it and his mouth thinned. 'I'm afraid not. I was just coming back from escorting my friends to their cars when I saw you. But as I said, your virtue is quite safe from me,' he told her sarcastically, his eyes running over her in distaste.

His answer made up her mind, and his eyebrows again went up in surprise when she said, 'All right, I'll come with you,' and began to walk quickly down the quay again.

Catching her up, Crispin Fox said, 'It's just a little

further on,' and saved Tressy from giving away that she already knew which was his boat.

He led the way on board, and she saw that it was as luxuriously equipped and furnished as she had expected. 'You can change in here,' he told her, opening the door to what must be a guest cabin from the unmade-up bunks. Tressy hesitated in the doorway and he gave a thin smile. 'You'll find a bathrobe hanging in the wardrobe. And if you want a shower, the bathroom's next door. Give me a call when you're ready and I'll put your things in the washing machine.'

Tressy nodded and went into the cabin, firmly closing the door and locking it. And if he heard, she didn't much care; she felt safer with the door locked. She took her dress off quickly, worried that it might already be permanently stained, and found, as she had feared, that the whisky had gone right through to her bra and pants. She took those off, too, recoiling from the strong smell, and looked in the wardrobe he had indicated. She found the bathrobe straightaway, a very thick expensive one in a rich wine colour with an Yves St Laurent monogram on the pocket. Putting it on, she found that it was only a little too large for her, so it was a woman's robe and not a man's. So what did that tell her about Crispin Fox?

Coming out of the cabin, she remembered just in time that she wasn't meant to know his name and called out, 'Hey, are you there?'

He was in the galley, stacking glasses, and came out to take her things, his eyes running dispassionately over her.

'I'll take that shower now,' she said.

He nodded. 'Okay. You'll find clean towels in there.'

Tressy took her time, enjoying the novelty of her

surroundings, the compactness of the shower room, which, although very small, was fitted with every luxury it could hold. She delighted in the foaming shower gel and gorgeous soft sponge, the mirrors that didn't mist up, and the huge soft bath sheet that covered her from neck to toes and went round her twice. Crispin Fox certainly knew how to spoil himself, she thought as she smoothed expensive body lotion into her skin. If Nora married him she wouldn't want for a thing—not that she did already. But Nora and Crispin Fox? She shook her head at herself in the mirror. She just couldn't see it. No way could they ever make a match of it, they just weren't compatible. Tressy combed her hair, tied the robe tightly round her and went to find him.

He was sitting out in the cockpit, smoking a cigarette and reading a newspaper which he put aside when he saw her. It was a perfect night, with a moon that dappled the sea and lit flames in her red hair. Tressy glanced up at the sky and then round at all the boats, hardly moving in the sheltered waters of the harbour, many of them with lights in the windows. The sound of gentle music from a boat further along covered the noise of traffic and it seemed very peaceful, a far cry from what she was used to in London. She gave a small sigh, then turned, reluctantly, to face Crispin Fox.

His eyes were on her, the cigarette temporarily forgotten, but when she turned round, he said, 'Would you like a drink?'

For a moment she thought of refusing, but then tossed her head rather defiantly. Why not? 'Thanks, have you any Campari?'

'I think so.' He stood up. 'Sure you wouldn't rather have whisky?'

Glancing at him quickly, Tressy saw the mocking

look in his eyes and gave a small smile in return. 'Campari will be fine.'

She sat down on one of the cushioned seats, carefully tucking the bathrobe round her legs so that it wouldn't come open, then saw an amused smile on Crispin Fox's lips as he watched her. Damn him, he knew darn well that she hadn't any underclothes on! She glared at him indignantly, but it only seemed to increase his amusement. Then he went inside to get her drink.

When he came back, he also carried one for himself. Tressy guessed that he must have had quite a few drinks during the course of the evening, first with his friends, and then with Nora and her parents, and now with her, but it didn't show at all, he appeared to be completely sober.

'Cigarette?' He offered her a packet, but Tressy shook her head and he sat down again, across the other side of the boat. For a while he watched her as she sipped her drink, perhaps waiting for her to speak, but when she didn't broke the silence by saying 'Perhaps we should introduce ourselves. My name is Crispin Fox.'

Her name was the last thing Tressy wanted to tell him. 'Did you put my dress in the washing machine?' she demanded abruptly.

His face hardened at her rudeness. 'Of course.'

'But did you make sure you put it on the right cycle? If the water's too hot it could shrink,' she reminded him anxiously.

'I followed the instructions on the label,' he answered coolly. 'Presumably that was correct?'

'I suppose so,' she said ungraciously. 'How long will it take?'

'Not long. And fifteen minutes in the tumble dryer should be sufficient to dry it.'

'You have a dryer as well on this boat?' Tressy asked in astonishment.

'Oh, we have all modern conveniences,' he replied laconically. 'Just like a house.'

She looked at him rather resentfully; her house didn't have either a washing machine or a dryer, either she or her mother having to walk the mile to the nearest launderette carrying the heavy bags of washing every week.

'Are you in a hurry to get home?' he asked her. 'Do you have to be in by a certain time?'

'What? Oh, no.' She shook her head.

'Presumably you're here on holiday. With your parents—or someone?' he asked after a pause.

'No. I'm a . . .' She hesitated, wondering what and how much to tell him without giving away her relationship to the Sinclairs. 'I'm not on holiday. I'm working over here for the summer.'

'In Monaco?'

'No, a few miles outside. At Cap . . .' She picked up her glass from a small table and her eye fell on a visiting card with her uncle's name and the address of the villa on it. As she read it she took a drink and nearly choked.

'Is it too strong for you?' Crispin Fox asked, a mocking tone in his voice.

She coughed and shook her head. 'It just went down the wrong way, that's all.'

'Of course,' he agreed, but there was scepticism in his voice. 'You were saying: that you're working at . . .?'

'In Menton,' Tressy lied hastily, naming a town just past Cap Martin, near the Italian border.

'As an au pair? While you're on holiday from college or something?'

It was natural for him to assume that, she supposed,

when she had said that she was only here for the summer, but she didn't like him and she decided to let him know that he was slumming—if he didn't think so already. 'Oh, nothing so posh. I'm just a maid in a hotel. I clean the guests' rooms, sort out the dirty linen and scrub the kitchen floor,' she added for good measure.

'Really?' She had expected him to look down his handsome nose and was rather disappointed when he didn't. 'And you're English. Why come all the way to France to work?'

'I like the sun,' she answered sharply, wanting to drop the subject.

But, 'I'm surprised you were able to get a work permit,' Crispin remarked blandly.

Tressy looked at him suspiciously, but his face was completely impassive and it was impossible to tell whether he was being sarcastic or not. Finishing her drink, she set it down on the table, covering Uncle Jack's card, then asked, 'The name of your boat—what does it mean?'

'*Chimera?*' He pronounced it Kymera. 'It comes from Greek mythology and means a fantastic idea, a castle in the air, if you like. It does have another less happy meaning, but that's the one I named the boat after.'

During their conversation the soft, liquid whine of the washing machine had sounded in the background, but now it stopped and Crispin Fox stood up. 'Sounds as if your things are finished; I'll put them in the dryer.'

Tressy let him do it; she wasn't going to jump up and offer to do it instead just to save him trouble. He stepped down into the cabin, and as soon as he was out of sight, she picked up Uncle Jack's card from under her glass and tossed it over the side; it was a relationship she definitely didn't want to encourage. Since she had seen Crispin Fox her feelings had changed completely, from wanting to help Nora to being absolutely dead against it, sure that her cousin would never find real happiness with him, even if something did come of it. But from the way he had recoiled when he saw the Sinclairs walking *en masse* along the quay, it was quite possible that she was also doing Crispin a favour by disposing of the card.

'The stain seems to have come out of your dress okay.'

She hadn't heard him come back and she jumped guiltily. 'Oh. Good.' He was standing in the cabin doorway, looking down at her, and she didn't like it or the way he was looking at her. Getting to her feet, she moved across the cockpit, away from him. 'Do you ever take the boat out, or is it just a stationary status symbol?' she demanded, resorting to rudeness because he made her feel ill at ease.

'What exquisite manners you have,' he observed sardonically, crossing his arms and leaning back against the bulkhead. 'Tell me, are you like this to everyone, or is it just me you've taken a particular dislike to?'

Tressy flushed and was glad her face was in shadow so that he couldn't see it. 'I don't intend to crawl to you just because you've got money, if that's what you mean. Although I suppose that's what you're used to,' she added jeeringly.

'No, it isn't what I meant,' Crispin corrected her, his voice hardening. 'It's possible to have self-respect whatever your position in life, so long as you do your job to the best of your ability. But you seem to have a chip on your shoulder a mile wide.'

'I'm not jealous of your money,' Tressy retorted hotly.

'But you're the one who brought up the subject,' he pointed out.

Goaded, she blurted out, 'Well, maybe it's just your type I don't like.'

'Oh?' He straightened up and moved slowly towards her until he was only a few inches away, his eyes daring her to be rude again. 'And just what is my type?' he demanded menacingly.

Cornered, Tressy said the first thing that came into her head, so maybe it was even the truth. 'Male,' she answered acidly.

'What?' His eyebrows flew up in astonishment. 'Don't tell me you're a man-hater? No, I don't believe it. You couldn't be—not with that face and that figure.' His eyes went over her body appraisingly and returned to search her face. 'No way,' he told her decidedly. '*You're* the type who can twist men round their little finger. Some men,' he amended.

'But not you?' Tressy couldn't resist asking, because he had left himself wide open to it.

He grinned, and she realised that she had also left herself wide open to any scathing remark he cared to make, and she tensed to retaliate, but he surprised her by merely giving a brief nod. 'As you say—not me.'

Feeling that the whole conversation was getting out of hand, she tried to end it by saying, 'Would you mind seeing if my dress is ready yet? It should be dry by now, surely.'

Crispin's grin widened and he shook his head at her in mock disillusionment. 'Now you've disappointed me.'

Tressy looked at him suspiciously. 'Really? Why?'

Reaching out a hand, he put a finger under her chin and lifted her head so that she was looking directly into his face, his dark eyes full of mocking amusement. 'Never start something that you can't finish. And especially something that you know you're never going to win,' he added derisively.

Angrily she jerked her head away and marched past him down into the galley section. The spin-dryer was still going round, but she switched it off and jerked the door open, taking her things out before it had even stopped spinning properly. Her dress was still a little bit damp, but she locked herself in the cabin and pulled it on in a rage. The insufferable man! Just who the hell did he think he was? My God, any woman with any sense at all ought to enter a convent for life rather than have anything to do with him. And as for Nora marrying him ... Tressy shuddered at the thought and determined to rescue her cousin from her own folly. Even if Nora didn't thank her now she was bound to later when she got over this schoolgirl crush she'd got on him. For that was all it could be, had to be.

The damp dress clung to her a little, but Tressy didn't notice, although Crispin obviously did when she strode on deck, her face stiff with scarcely controlled anger.

'Couldn't you even wait five minutes for it to dry?'

Tressy didn't even bother to reply, just collected up her bag and made for the gangway, but found him barring her way. 'Do you mind?' she demanded shortly.

'Going somewhere?'

'Home.' She glared at him.

'But haven't you forgotten something? I'm paying for the taxi.'

She had forgotten, and now she wished whole-heartedly that she could afford to tell him what to do with his taxi fare. But the last bus had gone and it must be a walk of several miles to the villa. For a moment she toyed with trying to hitch a lift, but she

didn't fancy risking it at this time of night in a foreign
country. Crispin's lips thinned into a crooked grin as he
watched her, almost as if he was reading her thoughts.
And he deliberately waited for her to concede.

'Damn you! Why the hell did it have to be you?'

He laughed and looked down at her mutinous face,
caught in the light of a nearby lamp. 'Your eyes are all
wrong,' he remarked, completely throwing her.

'Why, what's wrong with them?' Automatically she
lifted a hand, thinking that her mascara had run.

But her hand stilled as he said, 'They're blue. They
ought to be green with that shade of hair—and your
kind of temper,' he tacked on mockingly, to let her
know it wasn't a compliment.

Tressy bit her lip and held out her hand. 'If you'll
give me the money for the taxi, then I'll go. You
obviously don't want me around any longer, and I
certainly don't want to stay. As far as I'm concerned
the sooner I see the last of you, the better!'

'But meeting you has been quite an experience.' He
made no attempt to give her any money and Tressy
lowered her hand, feeling ridiculous.

'You mean meeting one of the working class?' she
asked scathingly. 'The other half?'

'Oh, but I work for my money, too, you know.'

'Humph!' Tressy gave a snort of disbelief.

'No, I meant that of all the girls there are on the
Riviera at the moment I had to run into you. A crazy,
mixed-up female who doesn't even have the grace to
be polite,' he told her disparagingly—adding cruelly,
'Who deliberately takes her bitterness out on complete
strangers. I don't know which man got to you or what
he did, but you're going to develop into an even worse
shrew if you don't soon learn to grow up and face
reality,' he finished grimly.

The colour had drained from her face, but

somehow, probably just as a silent denial of his accusations, she managed to hold on to her temper. Pushing past him, she strode across the gangplank and hurried down the quay towards the town, hardly aware of where she was going. So mad that she wanted to hit out at somebody.

There were some taxis waiting in the Boulevard Albert at the end of the quay. Tressy saw them, but turned in the other direction, intending to start walking to Cap Martin, but Crispin Fox caught her arm and pulled her to a stop. 'There's a taxi over there.'

'Let go of me!' Tressy furiously tried to shake him off. 'I don't care if I have to walk all the way home, I'm not going to take a penny of your beastly money from you!'

'So you've a little pride at least.' He swung her round to face him and saw that her eyes were wet. His voice softened as he said, 'Come on. You can't possibly walk all that way.' And he began to draw her towards the cab rank.

'You go to hell, Fox!' She tried to fight him off. 'I don't want your lousy charity.'

Keeping a firm hold on her arm, he whistled at the leading taxi and it drove over, the driver looking at them with interest. 'Take the lady to Menton. What's the name of your hotel?'

'Let go of me, you rotten beast!' She tried to kick him as he opened the taxi door and propelled her inside.

'Tut, tut, such temper! She'll tell you the name of the hotel when you get going,' he told the driver, passing over several notes. 'This should cover it.' He still held her arm, but now he pushed her right inside. 'Goodbye, you little vixen. You know, you never did tell me your name.'

'Mind your own damn business!' Tressy slammed the door and he had to jump back out of the way, but the effect was spoiled a little because the window was open, and she heard him laugh. 'You're the most horrible man I've ever met,' she declared passionately. 'And if I never meet you again it'll be too soon!'

His face hardened at her nastiness. 'And that goes for me too,' he assured her with feeling.

The taxi pulled away, but Tressy didn't look back. She was so mad at the way Crispin Fox had treated her that she could cheerfully have strangled him. For a few lovely minutes she indulged in all the things she'd like to do to him and thought now, too late, of all the things she could have said, but then the driver interrupted this pleasant occupation by asking where she wanted to go.

'What? Oh.' She gave him the address of the villa.

'Not Menton, *mademoiselle?*'

She shook her head, and he shrugged and turned back to concentrate on his driving. It was gone two o'clock, but there was still plenty of traffic about and lots of the cafés in the town were still open, but things quietened down as they left Monaco and took the coast road to Cap Martin.

Thank goodness she'd never have to see him again, Tressy thought. Keeping her promise to Uncle Jack was going to be the easiest thing in the world, and she would do her best to make sure Nora saw as little of Crispin as possible, too. Throwing away that address card might do some good; though she had to admit that someone of Aunt Grace's social ambition and pushiness wouldn't be put off when Crispin Fox didn't phone or return their visit. But it might give Tressy a little leeway, and in that time she would have to try and turn Nora's thoughts on to other things.

She was still trying, in vain, to think of something

that would distract Nora from her fascination for Crispin when the taxi pulled up at the entrance gates to the villa. She got out and turned to thank the driver, to find that he was holding some money out to her.

'The extra. To Menton. This is what you arrange, no?'

So he thought she'd given the false address to get some money out of Crispin. But she'd meant it when she'd said she didn't want his money. Drawing herself up, she gave an airy wave of her hand and said loftily, 'You keep it.'

Feeling better after her grand gesture, Tressy walked down the steep driveway to the villa, only to be met by an irate aunt and uncle who demanded to know where she'd been and whether she knew what the time was. But she had no fear of her relations and had had just about as much as she could take already tonight, so she immediately hit back.

'Look, let's get this straight. You may be paying me, but what I do and where I go in my own time is my affair and nothing to do with you. And if you don't like that arrangement you can put me on the next plane back to England for all I care. I didn't want to come here in the first place and it would suit me just fine to go home!'

That home truth took them back a bit, and it was Aunt Grace who was the first to say, 'There's no call to talk like that. We were worried about you, that's all. We thought you were in bed and your uncle would have locked and bolted the doors if I hadn't happened to look in your room to ... Well, I saw you weren't there and we didn't know where you'd gone or anything. I think you should have had a bit more consideration than going off like that without a word. What would you have done if you'd been locked out?'

'Rung the bell until one of you came to answer it,' Tressy answered honestly.

'Well, really!' Her aunt was affronted. 'In future you must tell us if you're going out and what time you'll be back.'

Tressy shrugged impatiently. 'It should be easy enough to devise some way of letting each other know whether we're home or not, surely?'

'Aye, but what I want to know is what you were doing eating the caviare and drinking a bottle of my best Burgundy?' her uncle demanded with red-faced annoyance.

So that was why her aunt had come to her room, Tressy guessed, to tell her off for taking the luxury stuff. Opening her eyes wide in feigned innocence, she said, 'Oh no, Uncle Jack, It wasn't your *best* wine—I made quite sure of that. I didn't touch the new stuff, I was careful only to take the oldest bottle I could find.'

Her uncle nearly choked and looked at her suspiciously, not knowing whether to believe her or not, but she returned his gaze blandly, and he muttered, 'My God, only took the oldest bottle she could find! Remind me tomorrow, young woman, to teach you about wine.'

'And caviare,' his wife put in.

They let her go then, and Tressy ran up to her room. She had intended to iron her dress before she went to bed, but she felt suddenly dog-tired. It had been a hell of a long day, what with the travelling and everything. After cleaning off her make-up, she collapsed into bed, her last waking thought one of acute dislike for Crispin Fox.

Nora was up almost an hour before Tressy was the next morning; another residue of her convent school upbringing. Tressy came awake with a groan, but the reflection of the sun coming through the only window in her room, so high up that she couldn't see out without standing on a chair, immediately beckoned, so she put on a bikini and ran down to the garden for an early morning swim.

Her cousin was already in the water; she was a good swimmer and was doing one length after another in a businesslike crawl, her swimming hat encrusted with plastic flowers bobbing through the water. Tressy, however, thought that pools were to be enjoyed and splashed happily about in the shallow end, getting in Nora's way when she wanted to turn. Eventually Nora gave up and came to sit beside her on the edge, where she was dabbling her feet in the water and lifting her face to the sun.

'Forty lengths,' she told her, out of breath, but with some pride. 'I have to do forty lengths every day to keep in shape.'

Tressy looked at her dispassionately. 'The only thing you're going to shape is your shoulder muscles. You don't want mannish shoulders, do you?' she said accusingly.

'Well, no.' Nora looked taken aback. 'But I want to keep slim.'

'But I'm slim, and you don't see me doing forty lengths a day.'

'You're naturally slim,' Nora said enviously. 'It's easy for you. I bet you've never had to diet.'

'No, but then I work very hard,' Tressy pointed out tartly, refusing to feel any sympathy for the other girl. 'Come on, let's go and have some breakfast.'

The maid who was part of the villa package had arrived and laid breakfast on a table on the terrace overlooking the superb view across the bay. The two girls went over, Tressy looking at the hot rolls and croissants with pleasure, Nora with dismay. 'I'll just have fruit juice.'

'One roll or croissant won't hurt you. Try one, they're delicious,' Tressy told her with her mouth full. 'I'm so hungry—aren't you?'

'Well, yes, but . . .' Hesitantly Nora reached out and took a croissant, glancing behind her to make sure her mother wasn't around. 'Perhaps just one.' She spread butter and marmalade on it and then ate it with obvious enjoyment, savouring each mouthful. Tressy grinned inwardly, thinking that Nora's love for food would probably prove to be greater than her crush on Crispin Fox.

'How did you get on last night?' she asked casually, helping herself to a roll. 'Did you run into this man you're chasing?'

'I'm not chasing him,' Nora said defensively, then, 'Well, yes, we did see him, actually.'

'Really? Where, at the Casino?'

'No, as a matter of fact it was on his boat,' Nora admitted uncomfortably, but then she went on eagerly, 'He was really nice to me. And he took us all over his boat, showed us everything. It's a really super boat, Tressy, you'd love it.'

Hastily lowering her eyes, Tressy said, 'He was pleased to see you, then?'

'Oh yes. Even though there were other people there. He gave us a drink and we stayed until his friends had to leave. We would have stayed longer, but he said he'd walk us down to our car at the same time,' she added naively.

So *that* was how he'd got rid of the Sinclairs so quickly. 'Who were these friends?' Tressy picked up another hot roll and spread it thickly with butter and honey, holding it near Nora so that she could smell that lovely new bread smell. 'Want half my roll?'

Nora gulped and almost drooled, but she shook her head determinedly. 'No, thanks. His friends? They were all French—a man and two women. The man had a *de* in his name—Michel de Quebris. That means he comes from an old aristocratic family, don't you think?'

'I suppose so,' Tressy agreed without interest. 'Who were the women?'

'I can't remember their names, but they weren't married. They were very smart,' Nora recalled wistfully, then brightened. 'I was glad I was wearing my new dress.'

'When are you seeing him again?'

'Mummy invited him to have dinner with us tonight, but he said he already had tentative engagements for the next few days and didn't know when he'd be free. So he's going to phone and let us know if he can come to lunch one day instead.' The disappointment was heavy in her voice. 'But Mummy also invited him for a party and asked him which day he was free, so he'll have to come for that,' she told Tressy gleefully, her mood immediately changing. 'It's in two weeks' time, on the Friday. What do you think I should wear? Or maybe I can get a new dress in Monte Carlo. There are some gorgeous shops there. You ought to see them.'

'I did. I went into Monte Carlo myself last night.'

Nora looked at her in astonishment. 'Alone? But how did you get there?'

'By bus, of course. You know, one of those long noisy vehicles with all the windows in the side that the common herd pay to squash into.'

'All right, I know what a bus is.' Nora was immediately offended. 'I just thought it was daring of you to go by yourself, that's all.' She chuckled. 'Daddy was as mad as fire when he came home and found the remains of your meal on the table. Caviare and his best Burgundy! He nearly hit the roof.'

The two girls grinned at each other, for once in sympathy.

Tressy stood up. 'Come on, there's something I want to do and you may as well come with me.'

'Where are we going?'

'You'll see. We'll go and change and I'll meet you by the front door. Oh, and bring some money with you.'

Nora went off to her room happily enough, and Tressy laughed as she changed into shorts and suntop. Whether she liked it or not, Nora's liberalisation was about to begin.

CHAPTER THREE

TRESSY had noticed the place she wanted the previous day, a small garage less than half a mile from the villa on the main road, with a 'For Hire' sign outside it.

'You're going to hire a car?' asked Nora with astonishment and some admiration in her tone as they turned into the garage.

But Tressy looked at her scornfully. 'How could I possibly afford to hire a car? Anyway, I can't drive. No, there's only one way to get around in the south of France. We're going to hire one of those.' And she pointed to a row of brightly-coloured motor-scooters standing ready for hire.

'A scooter? But can you drive one?'

'Any fool can drive a scooter,' Tressy informed her confidently, ringing the bell outside the garage.

'What did you mean, *we're* going to hire one?' her cousin asked with mounting alarm. 'You don't think I'm going to go on it, do you?'

'For heaven's sake, Nora!' Tressy's eyes widened indignantly. 'I'm only getting one for your sake. You don't want to go trailing around behind your parents the *whole* time, do you? You want to be free some of the time, surely?'

It hadn't occurred to Nora before that she wasn't free, but Tressy had put it so forcefully that she automatically nodded and said, 'Yes, I suppose so.'

'Good.' Tressy turned as an attendant came out on to the forecourt, wiping his hands on a cloth, his shoulders straightening as he ran his eyes over them in a way only a Frenchman can achieve. '*Bonjour,*'

Tressy greeted him, making her only concession to the fact that she was in a foreign country. 'We want to hire a scooter.'

'*Mais oui, mademoiselle.*' He brought two or three for them to look at, and Tressy prudently chose one that wasn't too powerful.

'We'll try that one.'

'*Bien.* I give you the lesson, no?' He demonstrated how the bike worked, then found them a couple of crash helmets and took Tressy out on the road, sitting behind her on the pillion seat with his arms round her waist and enjoying himself hugely as he shouted instructions in her ear.

'Okay, this one will do,' she told Nora when they got back to the garage. 'Pay the man, will you? Although he ought to be paying us, the way he was pawing me.'

With a resigned shrug, Nora did as she was told, refusing with horror the attendant's offer to take her for an instruction drive as well. 'Are you sure you can drive it?' she demanded anxiously when the man had gone.

'Of course. It's dead easy.'

'That's what I'm afraid of,' Nora observed gloomily.

Tressy turned to stare at her. 'My God, Nora, you made a joke! Maybe there's hope for you yet. Come on, put your crash helmet on and let's go.'

They wobbled a bit as they set off and Nora clutched her nervously, which didn't help, but Tressy managed to stay upright and carried on down the main road to Monte Carlo. Luckily it was that in between time for traffic; the working people had reached their destinations and the holidaymakers weren't yet in full flow. They got lost in the maze of streets and underpasses around Monte Carlo, so Tressy stopped to buy a street guide and a drink, which both of them needed badly. Tressy wouldn't admit it for a thousand pounds, but trying to drive for the first time after only twenty minutes' instruction, on some of the most congested streets in France and on the wrong side of the road thrown in, had been quite a nerve-racking ordeal. Her clothes were sticking to her and her hands were clammy with sweat.

'You can drive on the way back,' she offered.

Nora's face blanched. 'Oh no, I couldn't—I couldn't possibly. You'll have to do all the driving. Please, Tressy!'

'Oh, all right, if you insist. But I think it's a bit unfair making me do all the work. Tell you what, though; if I have to do all the driving, then you can pay for the petrol. That's fair, isn't it?'

'Yes. Yes, certainly. That's quite fair,' Nora agreed hurriedly, knowing it wasn't, but relieved to settle for it.

Several motorists had hooted at them or called out as they drove along, and for a while Tressy thought that she'd been doing something wrong, but as she gained confidence and it still went on, they realised that it was just because they were two girls on a bike, their skirts pulled up and showing a lot of leg. Nora didn't know whether to be pleased or annoyed.

When they got back to the villa they took off their helmets and hid them and the bike in an outhouse at the rear of the garage, where Nora's parents weren't likely to look.

'But why don't we just tell them we've hired it?' Nora objected, uneasy at deceiving her parents.

'Because they'll immediately forbid you to go on it, of course. And then you'll feel terrible when you *do* go on it,' Tressy pointed out with incontrovertible logic.

'But if they say I mustn't . . .'

'Oh, Nora, for heaven's sake! You enjoyed this morning, didn't you? And what harm was there in it? Why should you have to give up a simple pleasure like that just because they still look on you as a child instead of an adult?'

So Nora stayed silent when they went down to the pool where her parents were sitting and Tressy airily announced that they'd been for a walk.

'Our dresses from last night want pressing again. You could have done that this morning,' her aunt pointed out tartly.

'I thought I was supposed to be Nora's companion; I can't be in two places at once. But I'll go and do them now, if you like?' Tressy offered, thinking of her own dress that also needed ironing.

As she went inside, she heard Nora asking her mother eagerly, 'Has he phoned yet?' and gave a smile of satisfaction when Aunt Grace said, 'No, not yet, love.'

In the afternoon the three of them went for a drive in the car. As the maid didn't come in the afternoons, they left Tressy with strict orders to take very careful note of any phone calls, but as soon as they had gone Tressy went out into the garden to sunbathe and wouldn't have heard the phone even if it had rung. The next day Nora refused to leave the house in case Crispin rang, even though her mother tried to convince her that it was early days yet, and the poor girl got gloomier and gloomier as the hours passed. Tressy tried to persuade her to come down to the small beach at the foot of the promontory, but she wouldn't, she just sat in the shade of the terrace, within earshot of the phone. Refusing to feel in the least guilty, Tressy borrowed Nora's padded beach mat and went down to the narrow strip of beach, where she spread it on the pebbly sand.

One look round the beach showed her that every female in sight, whatever their age or shape, sunbathed topless. Tressy had never dared to do so before—if she'd tried it in England she would probably have been either accosted or arrested—but when in Rome . . . She started off by lying on her front, but by the end of the afternoon found it quite natural to be topless and would have felt overdressed otherwise. And it was lovely not to have to worry about strap marks all the time.

That evening her relations went to the Casino again in the hope of seeing Crispin Fox, Nora almost in tears because he hadn't phoned, so Tressy took the scooter as soon as they had gone and rode into Menton in the other direction. It was an older town, without the pretensions of Monte Carlo, its narrow streets crowded with people enjoying an evening stroll or eating in one of the many restaurants and ice-cream parlours. Tressy allowed a couple of good-looking French youths to pick her up and buy her a huge bowl of fruit and ice-cream and kept them at a distance by promising to meet them the next day with her cousin.

But the next morning, after her swim, Nora was even more fed-up than ever. 'We went down to the harbour to see if Crispin was on his boat,' Nora confided. 'But it wasn't there. He must have gone on a cruise. Daddy asked the harbourmaster, but no one seemed to know when he'd be back,' she said dejectedly.

Privately Tressy thought that Crispin had done the wise thing and was keeping well away, but she said bracingly, 'Well, you're not going to just sit moping around here until he deigns to turn up, are you? Surely you're not going to let it spoil your holiday just because he has the bad manners to not even ring? I certainly wouldn't if it was me. And quite frankly, I don't know what you see in him. Why chase some crabby old Englishman when you have all these gorgeous French boys to choose from?'

Stung, Nora retorted, 'He's not crabby!'

'He's thirty-two, isn't he? That's nearly as old as your father,' Tressy exaggerated.

'No, it isn't. And he isn't a bit like Daddy. He's— he's different,' her cousin said soulfully. 'You'd understand if you could see him. Or if you were in love.'

Tressy heaved inwardly at the sloppy look on Nora's face and said sharply, 'Well, he obviously isn't in love with you, or he'd have phoned days ago,' and then wished she hadn't, as Nora seemed about to burst into tears. 'Oh, I'm sorry, I didn't mean it. Look, why don't you come out with me tonight? I met these two really nice French boys last night and I told them all about you. They really want to meet you; they asked me to bring you with me tonight to make up a foursome.'

Nora brightened. 'They really want to meet me?'

'Yes. Definitely,' Tressy assured her. 'They like English girls and they thought you sounded terribly attractive.' If you're going to lay it on then lay it on thick, she told herself.

'Well, I don't know. If Crispin doesn't ring, Mummy and Daddy will want me to go to the Casino with them. And Crispin might be there.'

'It's hardly likely if his boat's gone. And anyway, you shouldn't run after him. Let him know other men find you attractive,' Tressy added the clincher.

They eventually agreed that if Crispin didn't phone, Nora would tell her parents she was tired, and when the two of them had gone out, she and Tressy would take the scooter and go into Menton, getting back before the Sinclairs returned.

Tressy gave a sigh of relief and satisfaction, glad that she was steering Nora's thoughts away from Crispin Fox. If she met some other boys and began to enjoy herself, she might forget her crush on him altogether.

She was kept busy all morning blow-waving Nora and her mother's hair before they all went out to lunch and then on into Nice to do some shopping. Ignoring their order to stay by the phone, she went down to the beach to sunbathe for a couple of hours, bought a few postcards, and then climbed the long flights of steps back up to the villa to find a pen and write them. That done, she searched the villa for some stamps, but Uncle Jack, the mean old skinflint, must have locked them away in his desk, which meant she'd have to go out and buy some. Tressy changed into a pale green dress that she'd bought in Menton the day before. All the young girls on the Riviera seemed to be wearing one like it; a simple sundress, but the skirt slit into long thin strips up to the thighs so that there were tantalising glimpses of your legs as you walked along.

Now that she was more proficient Tressy didn't bother with the crash helmet; hardly anyone did. More often than not they didn't bother much in the way of clothes either; she'd seen lots of young people driving along in just a bikini or a pair of swimming trunks. Revving up the bike, Tressy went off at a faster rate than she'd intended and shot up the steep, curving driveway towards the entrance. Only there was a car already coming down! A big gunmetal-coloured Rolls-Royce. And it almost filled the driveway! There was just a small gap to the right of the car and Tressy desperately headed for it, but the car driver swerved the same way and suddenly there wasn't a gap any more.

The front wheel of the scooter hit the Rolls and

Tressy was flung over the handlebars, over the low hedge that edged the driveway and into the garden on the other side, narrowly missing a tree trunk and ending up on her back on the soft ground below a pine tree, dazed and completely winded. She lay there, unable to move, dimly aware of a car door banging and then someone leaping over the hedge and running towards her.

It was a man. He called out, '*Etes-vous blessée?*' as he ran, and then went down on his knees beside her. 'Dear God, I . . .' And then in an entirely different voice as she tried to sit up, 'Good Lord, it's you!'

Tressy managed to bring her dazed eyes into focus and groaned—but it wasn't from pain. The man who was staring at her so incredulously was Crispin Fox. She groaned again and closed her eyes, counting to ten in the hope that she was hallucinating and he would have gone by the time she opened them, but the wretched man was still there.

'Are you hurt?' he demanded anxiously, putting an arm round her and helping her to sit up.

'I don't—think so. Just a bit dazed, that's all.'

'Don't try to move too much. Are you sure you haven't got any pain anywhere: in your legs or arms?'

'No. It feels okay.' But everything suddenly went giddy and she closed her eyes, leaning her head against Crispin's shoulder, hardly aware of what she was doing. After a few moments she opened them again and found him looking at her with concern in his dark-lashed eyes. 'I'm—I'm all right now.'

'Sure?'

She tried to nod her head. 'Ouch!'

'What is it?'

'My head hurts.'

Kneeling as he was, Crispin picked her up in his arms and got easily to his feet, carrying her down to the villa.

'Hey, I don't need to be carried. I can walk,' she protested.

'Shut up.' His arms tightened to stop her struggling until he set her down on a lounger on the terrace. 'I'll call a doctor,' and he moved towards the house.

'No!' Tressy exclaimed in alarm. 'It's not that bad—really.'

'But your head . . .'

'It's only a headache; I don't need a doctor for that.'

'You could have concussion. I'll get someone to phone. I'm not going to take the responsibility for your . . .'

'Well, I am,' Tressy interrupted crossly. 'It's only a bump on the head, for heaven's sake.' Tentatively she put a hand up to touch it, and winced.

Crispin Fox, his fears relieved, was suddenly and disconcertingly angry. 'And it serves you damn well right! If you'd been wearing a helmet you wouldn't have got a bump on the head at all. You behaved totally irresponsibly. You could have been killed!'

'Oh, did I?' Tressy got to her feet, her head temporarily forgotten. 'And what about you? If you hadn't swung right into my path I would have missed you completely. It was entirely your fault.'

His jaw jutting forward, Crispin said, as if talking to a backward child, 'It may interest you to know that this is France. People drive on the right-hand side here, and if you'd kept to the rule of the road we'd have missed each other, but you, of course, were on the left. I swerved in the opposite direction to that I thought *you'd* take.'

'Oh.' For a few seconds she was completely taken aback and could only say waspishly, 'Well, this is a private driveway and I shall use any damn side I like!' then sat down again rather hurriedly as her head started to swim.

Crispin looked down at her grimly and then over at the house. 'How do you know there isn't anyone in? And what are you doing here at the Sinclairs' villa anyway?' he asked in puzzlement.

Tressy could see all sorts of unpleasant explanations having to be made. 'Look, would you mind very much just going away and coming back again later? At about five-thirty, say.' A thought struck her. 'Oh hell, your car! I didn't do too much damage to it, did I?'

He dismissed it with a shrug. 'The car is of no importance so long as you're not hurt.'

Tressy stared up at him incredulously. 'God, if I owned a Rolls-Royce I wouldn't say it was of no importance,' she said feelingly.

Pulling up a chair, he sat on it the wrong way round, with his hands resting on the back. 'Just why are you so eager to get rid of me? And so reluctant to have a doctor?' he demanded, his eyes watching her keenly.

Tressy swallowed at what she knew was coming. 'It's an—er—long and involved story. You wouldn't find it at all interesting,' she assured him without much hope.

'Try me.' Taking a cigarette from his pocket, he lit it and looked ready to settle for the rest of the afternoon.

'Oh, hell!' She looked into his face, but his hard features were completely implacable. 'Well, if you must know, I'm staying here. Jack and Grace Sinclair are my aunt and uncle and Nora is my cousin.'

'Nora?' His eyebrow rose.

'Leonora.'

An amused glint came into his eyes. 'And you're on holiday with them? So why all that rigmarole about slaving away in a hotel?'

'No, I'm not on holiday,' Tressy snapped. 'They're

paying me to be a kind of lady's maid and companion to Nora. I'm just the poor relation, and therefore of no interest to you whatsoever.'

To her surprise he reached forward and caught hold of one of her hands, turning it so that he could look at her palm. There was a small blister from ironing, but apart from that her hand was quite soft. He didn't make any comment, just let it go. 'Did you know that I knew the Sinclairs?' he asked her. When she nodded reluctantly he went on, 'So why didn't you tell me who you were when you were on my boat?'

'It hardly matters, surely,' Tressy said uncomfortably. 'Look, I'll tell them you were here and . . .'

But he said insistently, 'You haven't answered my question.'

Tressy glowered at him. 'I didn't tell you who I was because—well, because I was supposed to keep out of your way.'

His eyebrows came up at that. 'Go on—what is your name anyway?'

'It's Tressy Sinclair.' She hesitated, not wanting to put her foot in it more than she could help, but he was waiting expectantly and she knew that eventually she'd have to tell him. With a hunted look, she said, 'Nora— well, she's got a bit of a crush on you. You must know that?' But he didn't even blink, and Tressy's voice grew cold. 'They thought they'd be seeing quite a lot of you and they decided it would be better if I kept out of the way.'

'So as to give Leonora a clear field?'

'Yes. Something like that,' Tressy admitted grudgingly, her dislike hardening. 'Anyway, I promised I would, so naturally I didn't want them to know that I'd met you.'

'So you gave me that load of lies?' He looked at her

sardonically and then asked the question she was afraid he'd ask. Trust him not to miss a thing! 'So what were you doing on the quay near my boat if you'd promised to keep away?'

Inspiration suddenly came to her and Tressy answered glibly, 'I knew that they were going to look for you down at the harbour, so I thought I'd find out whether or not they'd gone. I was hoping to get a lift back, you see.'

'Why weren't you on your scooter?'

'I didn't have it then; it was only our first day here.'

He seemed to accept the explanation and she gave a sigh of relief, but then realised that she now had to ask him a favour. Her mind rebelled at the idea, but there was no help for it. 'So I'd rather you didn't say anything about me meeting you before to the others,' she remarked as offhandedly as she could.

'No, I'm sure you'd rather I didn't.' Crispin grinned quite openly and Tressy could have killed him. 'You know, it could be quite interesting having you under an obligation to me. I must make sure that you repay it.'

Tressy flushed angrily. 'And just how do you propose to do that?'

The rotten man grinned maddeningly. 'Oh, I expect I'll think of something.'

Getting to her feet, she began to walk stiffly round to the front of the house. He was beside her at once. 'And where do you think you're going?'

'To move my scooter so that you can turn your car round and leave.'

He laughed softly. 'But maybe I don't want to leave. Perhaps I'll just wait until the Sinclairs get back.'

'Well, you can wait by yourself, then, because I certainly don't intend to waste my time talking to you any longer.'

'Temper, temper,' he remonstrated. 'Is that any way to entertain a guest?'

Tressy rounded on him angrily, ready to let fly and tell him exactly what she thought of him, but they had come round the house and she caught sight of the scooter lying almost under the wheel of the Rolls. The words died in her throat and she turned and walked slowly over to it, staring down at the scooter. 'The wheel's a bit bent,' she observed in a voice unlike her own.

'Mm.' Crispin stood the bike on its rest to examine it more closely. 'I might be able to do something about that.' Going to the back of the Rolls, he returned with a tool kit and began to straighten the wheel.

For a few moments Tressy watched him in silence, then said, 'I didn't think that people who owned Rolls-Royces did their own repairs.'

'Maybe they don't,' Crispin answered without looking up. 'But people who spend a large part of their leisure time on a boat can generally turn their hand to most things. There, that's better.' He spun the wheel with his hands. 'Where did you get the scooter?'

'From a garage on the road towards Monte Carlo.'

'Far away?'

'No, only about half a mile.'

'Well, you should be able to wheel it down there.' He straightened up. 'But *don't* try to ride it until you've had it checked, understand?'

'Yes, all right.' Tressy moved to push the bike out of the way, her hair falling about her face as she leaned forward.

'Maybe it would be a good idea if you took it along now. I'll come with you to explain in case you have difficulty with the language, if you like?'

'No, not right now. I'll take it tomorrow.'

Something in her tone caught his attention and he

took hold of her arm, reaching up his other hand to the side of her head so that she had to turn and face him. She was very white and there were goosebumps on her skin even though she was standing in direct sunlight. 'You're shaking,' he exclaimed. 'What is it—your head? But no, it must be delayed shock. You'd better come back to the house and sit down.'

He tried to lead her along, but Tressy shook him off angrily. 'I'll be okay in a minute. Leave me alone, can't you?' She turned her back on the scooter, trying desperately to control the stupid trembling in her limbs.

Crispin put his hands on his hips and looked at her exasperatedly. 'What the hell's wrong with you? Why can't you accept help when people want to give it?'

'I don't need any help.' Resolutely she swung round and grabbed hold of the scooter before he could stop her, and started wheeling it down the driveway to its hiding place.

'Why don't you keep it in the garage?' Crispin enquired, watching with interest as she stowed it away.

'And why don't you stop asking questions all the time?' retorted Tressy. 'It's none of your damn business where I keep it!'

'I see you've recovered,' he observed drily. 'You were almost polite when you felt ill. I suppose you hide it there because your aunt and uncle don't know about it?' The malevolent glare she gave him confirming that he was right, he went on, 'Does Nora know you have it?'

'Yes, of course she does. She's been on it.'

'Good grief, I gave her credit for more sense! You'll probably end up by killing the pair of you.'

'I don't usually drive on the wrong side of the road,' she told him tartly as she marched past him and back towards the front garden.

'Just how long have you been driving?' But Tressy ignored him and began to search round the hedge and bushes where she'd come off the bike. 'What are you looking for?'

'My bag. I dropped it when I—when you hit me.'

This retort received only a derisive, 'Ha, ha!' and then he said, 'You haven't answered my question; how long have you been driving?'

Tressy was leaning over the hedge, revealing a long length of very shapely leg through the slits in her skirt, but now she straightened up and said angrily, 'Oh, all right, three days, if you must know. I never drove before I came here.'

'My God, you're not fit to be let out!'

Her bag was hanging from a tree branch a couple of yards past where she'd landed. Tressy pulled it down and hastily took out her door key. 'I am going inside and I am going to shut the door, so you can either go or stay, I couldn't care less.'

Putting his head on one side, Crispin looked at her measuringly, and for a moment she thought he was going to meet her challenge, but then he gave a crooked kind of grin. 'What time did you say they'd be back?'

'About five-thirty,' she said with relief.

'And I suppose you'd rather I didn't say anything about the way we—er—ran into each other this afternoon either?'

Tressy squirmed, finding it almost impossible to find the words, and he said in mock sympathy, 'Hard, isn't it?'

'What is?'

'Having to ask someone to do you a favour.'

'It's hard asking *you*!' she burst out.

He grinned maliciously. 'But nevertheless you're going to have to ask if you want me to keep my mouth shut.'

'Ooh.' Tressy ground her teeth in frustrated anger. 'All right! I don't want you to tell them.'

'Please, Crispin,' he instructed.

She almost told him to get stuffed, but the thought of having to put up with her aunt's remonstrances for weeks on end held her back. 'Please,' she managed, and added when she saw his face, 'Please, Cris,' hoping that the shortening of his name would annoy him.

But he didn't seem particularly annoyed, merely saying, 'Hm, I suppose that's the best I can hope to get out of you. Okay, I won't tell them. And now I think you'd be well advised to go in and lie down.' He paused and gave a slight shrug. 'But then, if I tell you to do something, I've an idea you'll do just the opposite to spite me.'

'You're so right.' Tressy turned the key in the lock and stepped into the doorway.

He grinned at her mockingly. 'Most children are like that,' then laughed as she slammed the door in his face.

Nora's first question when they all got back about an hour later was the usual, 'Has he phoned?'

Tressy answered in the negative and her aunt looked at her suspiciously. 'Are you sure you've been here all afternoon?'

'Yes. As a matter of fact I was lying down with a headache,' Tressy assured her, thinking that a half truth was better than none.

She followed Nora into her room where her cousin had dejectedly dropped a pile of parcels on to the bed. 'What did you buy?' she asked.

'Not a lot. I didn't really feel like it. It's too hot to try on clothes. You can look if you like.'

'Wow!' The first parcel contained an Hermès beach robe in pale yellow towelling, as thick and soft as fur, with the Hermès monogram embroidered on the pocket just in case anyone didn't recognise it for what it was. And it had probably cost as much as her uncle paid her in a couple of months. Tressy ran her hands over it reverently; it was a beautiful thing and she longed to own one like it—who wouldn't? But she didn't envy it of Nora. Pale yellow was the wrong colour for her and would only make her look sallower; she should have had a deep red to give colour to her face.

Tressy unpacked the other things and put them away; doing her lady's maid bit. There was a lovely little evening bag, a pair of high-heeled sandals and a whole boxful of cosmetics.

'What do you want all these for?' she demanded. 'Once you get a tan you'll hardly need any make-up.'

'But Mummy says I must keep my face out of the sun. It said in one of her magazines that there was nothing worse for prematurely ageing the skin. And if you stay out in the sun too long you could get skin cancer.'

'Nora, if you listen to your mother you'll never do anything. What's the point of coming to a sunny country if you don't go out in it?' She caught the look on the other girl's face and said tartly, 'Oh, sorry—I forgot you only came here to chase Crispin Fox.'

'Well, I can hardly chase him if he isn't here, can I?' Nora returned with asperity. 'Still, we have got that date tonight, haven't we?'

For a moment Tressy toyed with telling her that the scooter was out of commission, but Nora wouldn't want to go out anyway when Crispin turned up, so she decided to let Nora break the date and be the one to feel guilty.

Her aunt called her and deliberately kept her busy for the next hour, cleaning shoes and generally running around. Tressy's headache grew rapidly worse and she even wished that Crispin would arrive to provide a distraction. But he didn't turn up until nearly seven, in the middle of a big row taking place upstairs between her uncle and aunt. As they'd arranged, Nora had announced that she was tired and didn't want to go out, and her mother immediately said that in that case they would all stay in, but her father was made of sterner stuff and protested that he wanted to go out to dinner and on to a casino they hadn't tried yet in the Avenue de Gaulle. They at once started to argue, Uncle Jack shouting out from his dressing-room where he continued to change, and Aunt Grace wandering backwards and forwards in her underwear not knowing what to dress for.

Tressy was the only one who heard the bell ring and put her head round Nora's door. 'There's someone at the front door.'

'Well, I can't answer it, I'm too tired,' Nora retorted from where she was relaxing on the bed, and laughed at Tressy's annoyance.

So then she went and banged on her aunt's door, trying to make herself heard above the noise they were making. Not one of them had shown any sympathy when she'd told them she'd got a headache, and now it hurt so much she wanted to scream. 'There's someone at the front door!' she shouted.

'Then go and answer it,' her uncle thundered back. 'That's what you're paid for!'

Tressy tried again. 'Aunt Grace, there's someone . . .'

'Well, I can't go, I'm in my underwear.'

The sound of the bell rang through the house again, impatiently this time, and Tressy groaned. No matter how much she tried to keep her promise to her uncle it seemed that she was doomed to break it. But this time it was his own fault, not hers. Resignedly she went downstairs.

'All right, I'm coming. You don't have to keep your finger on the doorbell!' she exploded wrathfully as she jerked the door open.

Crispin burst into laughter. 'Do they know how you open the door to their guests?'

'They haven't had any other guests.' She stood back to let him in and then stared. He wasn't alone, he'd brought with him the man she had seen on his boat, the Frenchman whose name she couldn't remember.

'I trust Mr and Mrs Sinclair are at home?' Crispin said smoothly.

'Why, yes.' Despite herself, Tressy was slightly overawed by their height and casually expensive evening clothes, both men in white jackets with bow ties at their necks. To counteract it she said, 'They're upstairs having a God-Almighty row. But don't worry, it will stop as soon as they know you're here.'

After showing them into the drawing-room, Tressy went upstairs again, realising that she was going to enjoy seeing her aunt's face. She banged on their door again and, after the second time, her aunt came to open it, red-faced from the argument that had progressed far past its original disagreement.

'Well, what is it? Why couldn't you have called through the door?'

'Because you were arguing so loudly; I could hear you all the way downstairs,' Tressy answered wickedly. 'I just thought you'd like to know that someone called Crispin Fox has arrived, and there's another man with him, a Frenchman.'

Her aunt's reaction was everything she expected it to be; she went first white and then red again, then she started to rush out in the corridor to go and tell Nora, but realised she was still in her petticoat and rushed back in again. 'Go and tell Nora,' she hissed at Tressy. 'Could they really hear us arguing downstairs? Oh, Lord love us! What shall I wear?'

'Shall I stay out of the way?' asked Tressy.

'What? Have you offered them a drink? Well, go and ask them what they want. But tell Nora first. Oh, where's Jack? He'll have to go down to them,' she wailed. And then the door was slammed as she literally ran to dress.

Nora's reaction Tressy didn't like. She was instantly transformed, her eyes sparkling as she, too, ran to get ready, pulling clothes out of the wardrobe and throwing them aside as she tried to make up her mind what to wear.

As she went slowly back downstairs, Tressy realised that all her plans to distract Nora away from Crispin were useless now, she would take his coming here as a definite indication that he was interested in her. And perhaps he was. Why else should he call? Her face grim, Tressy went into the drawing-room and said coldly, 'They'll be down shortly. Would you like a drink?'

'Thank you.' Crispin's eyes lingered on her disapproving face and his lips curled in amusement. 'A whisky and soda for me, please. And for you, too, I think, Michel?'

His companion nodded and Tressy went over to the cabinet to pour the drinks. She was aware that both men were watching her: Crispin in that hatefully amused way, knowing that she didn't want him there, and Michel de Quebris in appreciative and interested speculation, guessing that there was something between them but not sure what it was. But she was saved from their further scrutiny when her uncle hurried into the room, apologising profusely for not being there to receive them and shaking hands in his bluff manner.

'Please, it's I who should apologise,' Crispin demurred. 'I would, of course, have phoned first, but unfortunately the card you left somehow got mislaid. And I probably wouldn't have been able to repay your call at all if you hadn't left that message with the harbourmaster.'

'It's lucky we did, then,' Uncle Jack laughed. 'We managed to get tickets for the theatre and wondered if you'd like to join our party.'

Tressy carried the drinks over to the two younger men and then turned to her uncle, but he just said curtly, 'That'll do. I'll get my own.'

She turned to go, but Crispin said clearly, 'But aren't you going to introduce us to this young lady?'

'Oh, but she's only the ma . . .'

But Crispin interrupted before he could finish, saying, 'She has a definite look of you, Sinclair. I wasn't aware that you had more than one daughter.'

Uncle Jack gasped and nearly choked, and Tressy had to hastily look away to stop herself from bursting out laughing; she and her uncle weren't in the least alike, thank God.

'She's not . . . She's not my daughter,' Jack Sinclair managed to stammer, his face bright red with anger and indignation.

'No?' Crispin questioned blandly. 'Some other relation, then? Your niece, perhaps?'

Tressy tried to catch his eye and frown him down, but he deliberately didn't look in her direction.

Uncle Jack got his voice back and said suspiciously, 'Has she said anything to you?'

Crispin's left eyebrow rose rather disdainfully. 'My dear chap, she merely showed us into this room. I take it, then, that she is a relative of yours?'

Knowing that he was cornered and that there was no way out, her uncle nodded and said ungraciously,

'She's my niece,' and would have left it at that if Crispin hadn't turned to her and held out his hand.

'How do you do, Miss . . .?' He turned questioning eyes to Jack Sinclair.

'Sinclair,' he supplied with annoyed reluctance. 'Tressilian Sinclair. She's my brother's daughter.'

'Tressilian; what an unusual name,' Crispin remarked as he shook hands with her, devils of amused mockery in his eyes. 'I hope you're enjoying your holiday?'

Tressy glared at him and tried to pull her hand away, but he held on to it as he led her over to his friend. 'May I introduce Michel de Quebris? An old friend of mine and a native Monegasque.'

'*Enchanté, mademoiselle.*' Michel gallantly took her hand and kissed it, and Tressy looked at him in some awe; only a Frenchman could get away with that in this day and age without looking like a ham actor.

Her uncle got himself a drink and, when he noticed Crispin's raised eyebrow, remembered to offer her one as well, which she refused. For a few minutes they stood and talked, Crispin deliberately drawing Tressy into the conversation so that she couldn't slip away as she wanted to and as her uncle was trying to get her to do with eye signals that he tried to hide from the others. Why Crispin had forced the introduction she didn't know, and the fact that he had made Tressy instantly suspicious. And why had he brought his friend with him instead of coming alone? Even though she disliked him so much, Tressy had to admit that she found his actions intriguing.

Aunt Grace and Nora came into the room together, Nora wearing a skin-tight white dress that might have looked good if she'd had a tan. She seemed to think that she ought to wear very tight dresses to show off her thinness, but it just revealed the hollows under her shoulder bones and made her look gawky. Also she had made up her face herself, probably using her new set of cosmetics with a liberal hand, but she had been in too much of a hurry, so that the result was overdone and amateurish, like a teenager let loose with stage greasepaint.

Her aunt didn't notice Tressy until after she had greeted the visitors, but then she turned on her while they were speaking to Nora. 'What d'you think you're doing here?' she hissed angrily. 'Get on out!'

Tight-lipped, Tressy moved to obey her, but as she got to the door, Crispin said, 'I wondered if you'd all care to have dinner with us tonight? Tressilian, too, of course.'

She stopped and turned to stare at him while Grace Sinclair said hurriedly, 'Oh, we'd love to. How very nice. But Tressy can't come.'

'Oh? Why not?'

'Because ... because...' Her aunt stood there helplessly, too flustered for a moment to think of an excuse.

'Because I have a headache,' Tressy put in clearly.

'That's right. She was lying down with a headache before we came home.' Her excuse was swiftly and eagerly corroborated.

Crispin's brows drew into a frown. Only he knew that she had more than true reason enough for a whopper of a headache. 'Have you eaten yet?' he asked abruptly.

Taken by surprise, Tressy automatically answered, 'No,' before she'd thought about it.

'Then I'm sure that your head will feel much better after you've had something to eat. But if it doesn't clear up, I promise to bring you straight back home,' he assured her.

All three Sinclairs were looking at him with

expressions that at any other time Tressy would have found funny: astonishment, resentment and uneasy apprehension chased across their faces.

'But she *can't* come,' Nora began to object. 'She's only here to . . .'

'Nora,' her father said in quick warning, 'I've already told them she's my niece.'

Unable to stamp her foot and throw a tantrum to get what she wanted, Nora had to resort to, 'But she isn't ready.'

'Then we'll wait,' Crispin said smoothly. 'I'm sure she won't be long.' Crossing to Tressy's side, he reached to open the door for her. She looked up into his face, trying to read some purpose behind this game he was playing, but his features were completely enigmatic. For a moment she hesitated, knowing that it was still within her power to refuse to go, but curiosity overcame her and she gave a mental shrug. After all, the cat was out of the bag now anyway, so what had she got to lose? And if Crispin Fox was paying for the meal she would make sure she had a good one. So she merely turned and ran upstairs to change.

Her tan, too, wasn't more than a pale brown as yet, so Tressy put on a simple black dress and jazzed it up with a colourful scarf tied round her waist and a jewelled band, gypsy-fashion, round her forehead. She didn't use much make-up, but she knew how to use it, and quickly, so that within twenty minutes she was ready, standing tall, slender and sophisticated to give a last critical look at herself in the long mirror in Nora's bedroom before going downstairs.

They were all talking away as she quietly entered the room, her aunt and uncle to Michel and Nora to Crispin, gazing up adoringly into his eyes, but first Crispin and then the others noticed her and fell silent.

Her relations had never seen her dressed up for the evening before and were surprised at the change in her, Nora most of all. She turned petulantly away, ignoring Tressy and speaking to Crispin again. He didn't seem to hear for a moment, but then he bent to courteously listen to her.

They left soon after, and while they were sorting out who should go in which car, Tressy momentarily found herself alone with Crispin. 'What the hell are you doing this for?' she demanded in an undertone. 'You promised you wouldn't give me away.'

'But I haven't,' he pointed out. 'We've now been introduced, so that I can know you officially.'

'Don't play games with me,' Tressy retorted. 'Why have you invited me to dinner?'

'To make the numbers up, of course,' he replied blandly, his face a picture of innocence.

Goaded, she opened her mouth to have a go at him, but Nora saw them together and came over to intervene.

'I'll come in your Rolls with you, Crispin,' she said with a smirk. Then, 'Oh, your poor car! There's a dent in the wing. Did you have an accident?'

'A kind of accident,' he agreed, adding with a sideways look in Tressy's direction, 'As a matter of fact, someone ran into me.'

Nora was immediately indignant. 'Well, I hope you make them pay for the damage.'

'Oh, I intend to,' he assured her. 'To the last centime.'

Tressy gave him a filthy look, aware now of how he was amusing himself at her expense, then strode angrily away to get in the back of her uncle's car and slam the door.

CHAPTER FOUR

CRISPIN took them to the Empire Room Restaurant in the Hotel de Paris, one of the most popular and famous places in Monte Carlo. It was a huge room, fabulously and ornately decorated in the Empire style with a long fresco painted all across one wall. Nora and Aunt Grace obviously hadn't been there before and exclaimed in admiration as the maître d', who recognised Crispin and knew his name, conducted them to their table, a good one near a window looking over a garden and the sea.

Tressy somehow found herself between Crispin and Michel, with Nora on Crispin's other side, although she had tried to manoeuvre so that she would be between Michel and her uncle, not wanting to give Nora grounds for further jealousy. How she had come to be out-manoeuvred she didn't quite know.

Michel began to tell them the history of the hotel, which was beside the Casino, describing how it was built to house the kings and queens, aristocrats and nouveaux-riches who flocked to the Casino when it opened in 1865. 'This is a beautiful room, *non*?' Michel asked her.

Tressy looked round and decided that it was too ornate for her taste, but remembered in time that her neighbour was a native of Monaco. 'I'm sure it was very fashionable in its time,' she answered diplomatically.

She could have sworn that Crispin chuckled beside her, but the sound was lost under Aunt Grace's gushing praise of the room. Tressy quickly turned to

74

look at him, but his attention was on the head waiter,
who had just come up to the table. The menu of
course was completely in French. Aunt Grace said
something in an undertone to her husband and then
they both looked at her, and Tressy guessed that they
were afraid she would show them up by ordering a
fingerbowl of water or the cover charge or something.
She was strongly tempted to do just that, just to spite
them, but Crispin's laugh made her change her mind,
aware that she was on trial in his eyes as much as in
theirs. Although she never bothered to use it, Tressy
had, along with everyone else, done French at school
and she recognised enough words to pick out the
basics of the dishes, and when she didn't understand
she simply asked the waiter who hovered deferentially
at her elbow. If you don't know something—ask, was
one thing at least that she *had* learnt.

Since that brief conversation by the car, Tressy had
been afraid that Crispin would pursue this game of his
by paying her too much attention, but he divided his
time equally between Nora and herself without
favouritism, and often drawing everyone into a general
discussion. He was a very good host, keeping his eye
on the way the meal was going and lifting a finger to
attract a waiter whenever he thought anyone needed
something. Tressy had to hang back a little on one or
two courses to see which of the large array of knives
and forks beside her plate she should pick up, but she
learnt quickly and enjoyed the meal, although she had
been thwarted in her intention to order the most
expensive dishes she could find by there not being any
prices on the menu.

The food was a real treat, she very seldom got the
chance to eat really good food and she savoured every
mouthful, finding that the French preferred to serve
smaller portions but of a very high quality. The wines,

though, were something else again. Tressy knew very little about wine except that it came in different colours, and she was bewildered by the way a new wine was brought for almost every course. My God, how the rich live, she thought, lifting her long-stemmed glass and watching all the hundreds of lights in the room reflected in its cut surface. She wondered if it was as much a treat for anyone else in the room as it was for her. Probably not. They all looked as if they lived to this standard every day of their lives.

Crispin turned towards her and, after a couple of minutes, said, 'Do you like it here?'

Withdrawing her eyes from her glass, Tressy shrugged indifferently. 'It's okay.'

'How's your head?'

'Not too bad.' She was surprised to find that he had been right and her head didn't hurt so much now that she had eaten. 'I suppose you eat here all the time?'

He shook his head. 'Very seldom. Only when I entertain people that I think might like this sort of ambience.'

Which gave her a good idea of his opinion of the Sinclairs' taste. Challengingly she said, 'I *don't* like it. It's too ornate and fussy. Everything's overdone.'

'So why didn't you say that when I asked you? Or is it just that you feel you have to challenge me all the time?' She didn't answer, just returned his gaze with animosity in her blue eyes. 'Why, Tressy?' he insisted.

'You know why, because your sort puts my back up,' she returned bluntly.

His mouth thinned. 'I'm not a sort, Tressy, I'm an individual. Try remembering that.'

Her mouth drew into an amused smile that didn't reach her eyes. 'I'd rather not bother to think about you at all.'

Instead of being offended, Crispin grinned at her.

'Be careful, I might decide to *make* you think about me.'

She laughed mockingly. 'You couldn't.'

'Now that sounds very close to a challenge.' His eyes were on hers, imps of devilment in their dark depths.

Tressy looked at him and was strongly tempted to pick up the glove he'd thrown her, but then she became aware of Nora watching her, and shrugged. 'You're crazy.'

'Coward!'

But again she didn't rise to his bait and turned to Michel, who was more than willing to talk to her after five minutes of Aunt Grace.

He was too long-nosed to be conventionally handsome, but he was a personable young man, with an attractive accent, and had been brought up to be charming to females of all descriptions, treating them as if they were very special and feminine. It was obvious that he was curious about her, but Michel was far too polite to come right out and ask her about her position in the Sinclair ménage or where she had met Crispin before. But that didn't stop him from trying to find out by asking subtle questions that would eventually give him the information he wanted. But Tressy decided to block him from the start, not wanting her aunt or uncle to overhear anything that might give her away. So she asked him instead about the Grimaldi family, Prince Rainier and his children, who ruled the minute but rich principality, and in this she struck gold, because he was a mine of information on the subject and immediately captured Nora and Aunt Grace's intense interest, and even Uncle Jack wasn't averse to all the name-dropping.

Tressy sat back in her chair, letting his voice wash over her. She had had too much wine after that knock this afternoon and felt decidedly lightheaded. The lights on the dozens of crystal chandeliers, the gold gilding on the walls, the silver cutlery and the jewels that sparkled on women's necks and wrists, were all too much for her eyes; she wanted to close them and shut out the glare. She felt dreamy, and too tired to talk any more, content to let her relations ask Michel the questions that kept him on the Grimaldi family. Again she wondered why Crispin had brought Michel along—because there was safety in numbers, perhaps? But there could be a perfectly innocent explanation, although she doubted it; somehow she couldn't believe that Crispin Fox would ever do anything innocently. But her poor old brain couldn't cope with the question and she let it go.

She was very aware of him sitting in the seat beside her, although there was plenty of space round the table and they hadn't touched at all. Through her half-closed eyes, Tressy could see his left hand lying on the table, a strong, tanned hand with long fingers and well-manicured nails. A ringless hand and one that wasn't used to manual labour, for all he'd said he could turn it to most things. He wore a watch on his wrist, a very thin gold digital watch that simply told the time and didn't have any gadgets, but still looked extremely expensive. Her eyes travelled slowly up his sleeve and she wondered whether his body was fit or flabby; he had been wearing a jacket on all the three occasions that she'd seen him. Tressy decided she was willing to wager a large bet on him being fit, he had that athletic kind of figure you only get from playing a lot of sport—or else working very hard, she thought wryly. Her eyes moved a little higher to his shoulders and then stopped abruptly as he spoke, and Tressy realised that she was, in fact, thinking about him even though she had told him she couldn't care less.

Quickly she looked away and became aware that Michel had stopped talking and her relatives were looking at her expectantly. 'Er—did I miss something?'

'Crispin has just asked us to go on to a night-club,' her aunt said impatiently. 'But I explained to him that you were tired.'

At any other time Tressy would have gone just to be perverse, but tonight she merely said, to her aunt's gratification, 'Yes, I am rather tired.'

'You'd be very welcome to come with us, you know that,' Crispin assured her.

Tressy lifted heavy-lidded eyes to his face and saw that he meant it. And from something in the back of his eyes she guessed that he knew she had been studying him, but she was in no state to care. She shook her head and then wished she hadn't. 'No, thanks. I'd rather go back to the villa.'

'Very well.' He looked at Michel over her head. 'I'll take Tressy home and then join you at Régine's.'

'No, no, you don't have to do that,' Uncle Jack said hurriedly when his wife elbowed him in the ribs. 'Tressy can take a taxi. There's no need to put yourself out for her.'

'But Tressy is my guest,' Crispin pointed out smoothly. 'I wouldn't dream of letting her go home alone when I have a car outside.' He pushed back his chair and stood up, put a hand under her elbow and helped her to her feet. 'I won't be long. Why don't you all have another cup of coffee before you leave?'

He gave Tressy only time to bid everyone a rather strangled, 'Good night,' before he shepherded her out of the restaurant, his hand firmly underneath her elbow. In the foyer he paused to sign his name to the bill and pass over several notes for extra tips, and then they were outside and the doorman was calling for his car.

Monte Carlo at night is an incredible spectacle, with its floodlit gardens and squares, and the streets where every other car is a Rolls or a Mercedes. Here the nightlife is the most highly organised on the Riviera, and probably in the world, with the exception of Las Vegas. As they drove along they passed flashing neon lights advertising gaming rooms or super-chic discos, cabarets and floor shows. It was an owl-town, one that truly came alive with the night.

But Tressy saw them only as a muddled blur and was almost asleep when Crispin pulled up outside the villa.

'Hey, you're home.' He gently reached out and ran a finger up and down her cheek to wake her.

'What?' She blinked and opened her eyes. 'This is a very smooth car,' she observed rather defensively.

'Are you all right?'

'Yes, of course I am. Thanks for the lift. 'Bye.' She got quickly out of the car and then had to hang on to the door for support. 'Oh!'

Crispin came quickly round the car to her side. 'Where's your key?' She gestured towards her bag and he fished it out for her, then stooped to pick her up.

But Tressy moved quickly if jerkily away. 'No! I can damn well walk.'

'Okay, so damn well walk.' But he put an arm round her waist to steady her and made sure she was leaning against the wall before he released her to open the door. 'Come on, I'll see you upstairs.'

'No, I can manage.' She looked up at him with troubled eyes. 'Look, I—I don't usually get like this after a few drinks. I'm *not* drunk. But I—just don't know what the hell's the matter with me,' she said fretfully.

'Have you been sunbathing today?'

'Why, yes, this afternoon.'

'Then that's probably it. Sunbathing and alcohol don't mix.' Taking her arm, he drew her into the house. 'You'll feel better tomorrow.'

'I can manage on my own now,' Tressy protested as he half-supported her up the stairs. 'Will you please let go of my arm?'

'No, so get used to the idea that you're going to be helped.' He pulled her roughly back when she tried to struggle free, stumbling and almost falling backwards down the stairs. 'For heaven's sake, woman!' As they reached the half landing he firmly picked her up to carry her the rest of the way.

Tressy glared at him as angrily as she could manage. 'This is the second time today you've carried me about—and I don't like it. So you can just put me down this minute. Those French tarts you play around with may go for all this he-man stuff, but it leaves me cold.'

'And who told you I go around with French tarts?' Crispin asked, quite unperturbed. 'Which is your room?'

Tressy looked rather swimmingly round her and put her arms round his neck, feeling unsafe even though he was holding her very securely. 'It's up on the next floor. Nora told me, she said you had two girls on your boat.'

'Well, how about you and Nora being the two girls on my boat?'

Tressy giggled. 'Nora isn't a tart.'

'Of course not,' he agreed. 'Are you?'

He paused and looked down at her, watching her intently. Tressy's eyes met his and she said slowly, 'So that's why you've come up to my room. You expect me to pay for my supper now, is that it?' She didn't struggle, just lay in his arms and stared up at him, her blue eyes as cold now as deep ice.

'Which is your room?' he asked.

For a long minute she was silent, then she said, 'The one at the end.'

He carried her inside and switched on the light, looking round the room and giving an exclamation of surprise at its smallness. Then he set her down on her feet, but kept his hands on her shoulders.

'Take your hands off me,' Tressy said very clearly.

Slowly he obeyed, his eyes on her face.

'Now get out. My body's my own, and I don't give it to a man just because he thinks he's paid for it,' she informed him, her voice arctic.

Deliberately Crispin put up a hand to cup her chin, running his thumb across her soft lips. 'You think you're so tough, don't you?' he said softly, 'But you're not tough, only brave. A kitten disguised as a tigress. I wish . . .' But he stopped abruptly. His tone changing, he said instead in a quite normal voice, 'Are you sure you can manage now?'

Tressy blinked, taken aback by his swift change of mood. 'Yes. Yes, of course.'

'I'll say good night, then.' He turned to go, but at the door looked round the room again with its spartan furnishings and tiny window. 'My God, couldn't they have given you anything better than this? It's more like a cupboard or a cell!'

Tressy had thought the same thing herself, but that was entirely different. Her hands balled into fists as she said forcefully, 'Don't you *dare* feel sorry for me! I don't need your pity. *Do you hear me?*'

Crispin's face grew grim and he covered the space between them in one swift stride. 'Very well, then, I won't.' Then he pulled her roughly towards him and kissed her hard on the mouth.

He didn't kiss her long enough for her to take fright and start to struggle, but released her after only a couple of minutes. His features still set into hard lines, he gazed down at her for a long moment, then turned quickly on his heel and walked out of the room, not even bothering to close the door behind him.

Tressy stood and listened to him going down the stairs, the front door closing and then the sound of his car driving away and mingling with the traffic noise from the main road. Then she sank on to her bed as if her legs had disappeared. Slowly she lifted a hand to touch her lips, and it was some time before she pulled herself together enough to undress and drop into bed, falling instantly into a deep sleep.

Towards morning her sleep grew lighter and she dreamed, but woke at around her usual time feeling completely recovered, but a bit vague about the night before. She remembered having gone out to the restaurant with the others and Cris giving her a lift home, and had the strangest feeling that he had kissed her, but decided that that was an impossibility and that she'd dreamt it; her mind was a kaleidoscope of half-remembered dreams this morning.

For once, Nora wasn't up before her and Tressy had the pool to herself. She lay on her back, floating on the surface, her hair spread out about her head like a fan. She had to admit that she had enjoyed last night; the meal was one she would never forget and it had been fun seeing how the other half live, but Tressy was basically a realist and knew that it had been a one-off evening, which was just as well, because it was the kind of lifestyle she could quite easily take to. Not that she need worry about getting used to it; her aunt and uncle would make sure that she was kept well out of the way in future. Tressy groaned and turned to swim to the side, not looking forward to having to face her uncle's recriminations. But it had been Cris who, for whatever reason, had invited her, she hadn't asked to go, and that gave her some defence. She reached the side and began to climb the steps. Her hair clung to her head, hanging long and straight down her back. Water dripped from her body which was already a pale gold and she wore only a pale blue bikini, darker now because it was wet. As she reached the top of the ladder and stepped on to the paved surround, she saw the maid crossing the grass towards her, and behind her was Crispin Fox.

As she saw him, Tressy instantly recalled that dream last night. It had been so vivid. But again she dismissed it; it couldn't possibly be true. He was looking at her intently, but when she lifted her chin at him, Cris gave a humourless smile and let his eyes run slowly down her wet figure in insolent appraisal before saying silkily, 'Good morning.'

Fully aware of his eyes and feeling virtually naked, Tressy said shortly, 'The others aren't up yet. You're too early.'

'You know, I thought the way I said good morning was quite polite. Would it be too much to ask for a civil greeting in return?'

'The way you looked at me just now wasn't civil!' Tressy flashed back at him as she went past him and sat down at the breakfast table.

He came and sat opposite to her. 'Touché. I admit it. The sight of you coming out of the water would gladden the eye of even old King Neptune.' He reached for a jug of orange juice and poured some into a glass.

'You are staying for breakfast, *m'sieur*?' The maid had been hovering nearby and looked at him uncertainly.

'Yes, indeed.' He smiled at the rather formidable-looking Frenchwoman. 'Could you be very kind and do me an English breakfast with two eggs and bacon?'

She smiled back, obviously charmed. '*Mais oui, m'sieur.*'

'I'll have that, too,' Tressy put in quickly, which made the smile slip a bit. 'And please tell Miss Sinclair that Mr Fox is here.'

The maid nodded and went away and Tressy looked across at Cris. '*Do* sit down and stay to breakfast, won't you?' she said with heavy sarcasm.

He grinned, not in the least put out. 'Are you always as nasty as this in the mornings?'

'Only with people I find objectionable and over-bearing,' she answered sweetly. But this sally had absolutely no effect, and he simply picked up a roll and started to butter it. 'Why did you ask me to go with you last night?' The question was out before she even knew she was going to ask it.

He ran his eye over her again, but critically this time. 'You looked as if you needed a decent meal; you're as skinny as a scarecrow.' But his eyes lingered on her hair which had started to dry and spring into soft curls.

'Thanks!' she said indignantly.

'That's quite all right. I knew you'd get round to thanking me for the meal eventually,' he added mockingly.

'I didn't mean . . .' Then she sank back in her chair. 'It was a good meal; I enjoyed it.'

'I wasn't sure you could remember.'

'Of course I remember. But I don't know if . . .'

'If what?' He gave her a keen glance.

Tressy shrugged and looked down at the table. 'Oh, nothing.'

'How are you feeling today?'

'Okay.' Then, rather antagonistically, 'I haven't got a hangover, if that's what you mean.'

'It isn't. Why do you always jump down my throat, even when I ask you the most innocent questions?'

'You're always asking questions. But you never answer any—not truthfully, anyway.'

He laughed and turned to compliment the maid as she laid a plate of eggs, bacon, tomatoes and even a sausage in front of him. Tressy only got half as much. She looked at his plate and then at her own and said bitterly, 'I suppose flattery gets you anywhere?'

'Stop moaning and get on with it, woman. You wouldn't have dared ask her for it if I hadn't come along.'

'Well, I'm certainly going to ask for it every morning in future. Mm, lovely!' She bit into the crackly bacon.

Cris raised an eyebrow. 'Even if you don't want it?'

'*Especially* if I don't want it.' Then she caught the look in his eyes and they both burst into laughter, the first time she had genuinely laughed since she'd known him.

It was rather unfortunate that Nora chose that moment to come through the French windows on to the terrace. They didn't notice her at first until Tressy looked round, the laugh instantly dying away when she saw the indignant fury on her cousin's face.

Cris turned, summed up the situation and got to his feet. Still smiling, he said, 'Good morning, Leonora. I hope you don't mind a guest for breakfast?'

'No, of course not. You're welcome any time, you know that.' As soon as he'd looked at her the frown had gone and she was all honey and sweetness. They shook hands and he pulled out a chair next to his. 'Tressy and I were just celebrating a victory,' he told her easily. 'We managed to get an English breakfast out of your maid. Would you like some? Shall I order it for you?'

'Oh, really? No, thank you,' she answered virtuously. 'I only ever have orange juice.'

Cris poured her some and chatted to her exclusively for a few minutes, restoring her to happiness again. She sparkled when he spoke to her, her face animated, but she had got ready in a hurry and it showed. Her hair wasn't combed through properly, there was a line of smudged mascara under one eye, and blue pearlised eye-shadow was all wrong for this time of the day.

'Did you come for anything special?' asked Nora.

'I did indeed.' He reached down to two white boxes that he had brought with him, one large and the other small. He gave Nora the large one. 'This is for you. And this for you.' He passed the much smaller one over to Tressy and she took it reluctantly, her eyes trying to read his face.

Nora opened her box eagerly and gave an exclamation of pleased delight when she took out a large spray of exotic lilies, bright yellow and orange. 'Oh, how super! Thanks awfully, Crispin, they're gorgeous.' She looked as if she would have liked to kiss him but didn't dare.

'I'm afraid they don't survive very long without water.'

'Oh, no. I'll go and find a vase at once.'

She ran indoors and Cris looked at Tressy. 'Aren't you going to open it?' he asked lazily.

'You don't have to give me presents.'

'I know. I wanted to.'

'Just because you give something to Nora doesn't mean that you have to . . .'

'Tressy,' he interrupted, 'I said I wanted to. Now stop being silly and open it.'

Her chin came up at that and sparks of anger flashed in her eyes, but she knew that Nora wouldn't leave them alone for long and she felt strangely averse to opening her gift in front of her cousin. So she slowly took off the lid and then gave a long sigh of awed reverence. The box contained a posy of white violets in a bed of damp moss, beads of dew still on their petals. Violets, violets in June. Tressy gently touched the delicate petals with the tip of her finger, marvelling at their perfection. She had never been given flowers before and a silly tear came to her eyes, even though she knew that they had only been given to her because Cris was too polite to leave her out. But oh, how much she preferred these tiny flowers to Nora's gaudy bouquet.

'Oh, violets. How sweet!'

She hadn't heard her cousin return, and now her disparaging voice made Tressy quickly blink and put the lid back on the box. She didn't thank him, she couldn't, just said a muffled, 'Excuse me,' and went inside as her aunt and uncle followed Nora on to the terrace.

Cris stayed for another half an hour or so, but Tressy kept out of the way. After finding a vase to put her violets in, she sorted out which of her aunt's and cousin's clothes needed to go to the cleaners and made up a load for the washing machine.

She was standing at the sink in the laundry room, washing the more delicate things by hand, when Nora marched crossly into the room. 'You've been invited to come out with us on Crispin's boat the day after tomorrow. He wants you to make the numbers up. Although why he's asked you when there are hundreds of girls of good family he could ask, I don't know,' she added rudely.

'I thought you were my family,' Tressy pointed out mildly. It was hot in the room and she lifted a soap-sudded hand to push her hair off her clammy brow.

'Well, you know what I mean.'

'Sure. You mean girls from rich families. I suppose you said I'd go?'

'We didn't have much choice really,' Nora admitted. 'Crispin more or less insisted. Perhaps Michel likes you, that could be it. And we knew you'd jump at the chance to go.'

'Did you, indeed? I've never been on a boat. I wonder if I'll be seasick,' murmured Tressy, tongue in cheek.

'Oh, Lord, I hope not! I hadn't thought of that.' Nora was horrified that Tressy would show her up. 'You'd better take some pills before you go on board.'

'Are you seeing Cris again today?'

'His name is Crispin,' Nora pointed out in her most upper class manner. 'No, I'm not. That's why he came so early; he's going to visit a friend and won't be back until late tomorrow.' She sat on a stool and looked at Tressy resentfully. 'I do wish you hadn't met him last night. I suppose he'll feel that he has to include you in everything now because you're part of the family.'

'Well, don't blame me; someone had to go and open the door. If you'd gone yourself I wouldn't have met him at all. Anyway, why don't you just tell him that I'm the paid help? He'd soon drop me then,' she suggested mischievously.

'But I couldn't do that!' Nora was horrified. 'He'd think we ... He wouldn't understand the circumstances,' she amended. She stood up. 'Have you nearly finished that? Mummy and Daddy are going into Nice to have lunch with someone they know and they're going to drop me off to do some shopping, so you might as well come with me.'

So Tressy spent the gorgeous afternoon trailing round behind Nora, watching her try on and buy clothes that didn't suit her, carrying her parcels and sweltering in the heat haze that came up from the pavement.

'Wouldn't you rather be on the beach getting a tan?'

she asked wistfully, as Nora sorted through a rack of evening dresses.

'No, I always go terribly red first.'

'I've got some super stuff that stops you from doing that,' Tressy assured her. 'And once you get a tan you won't have to wear make-up and you'll look much healthier.'

Nora turned on her, her patience, too, eroded by the heat. 'Will you for heaven's sake shut up? I don't *want* to look healthy.'

Tressy looked at her angry face, gave up and shut up.

But the next day she had more success and, when the older generation had gone out, persuaded Nora to come down to the strip of beach at the foot of the Cap to sunbathe by simply remarking on how sexy a tan always looked. Nora thought about that for a minute and then agreed to come. There were already many people there from other villas, or from nearby hotels, but they managed to find a space to spread their beach mats and put up a parasol that Nora had insisted on bringing. She seemed to think she needed a great deal just to spend a couple of hours on the beach and had a big bag full of absolute necessities.

'I don't know why we have to come down here when we could go on one of the private beaches in Monte Carlo,' she grumbled.

'Don't be so stuffy. This one's okay.' Tressy hadn't yet let on that she had damaged the scooter. She spread tanning lotion on Nora's back and legs, made sure that the parasol covered her head and found her book for her, then took off her own bikini top and lay back with a sigh of contentment, the sun fully on her.

Nora read quietly for about ten minutes, then turned to ask Tressy how long she'd had. 'Tressy!'

Her horrified exclamation startled Tressy out of her

semi-doze and she jerked up. 'What is it? What's happened?'

'You haven't got any top on! Cover yourself up.' Nora was carefully averting her eyes and holding out a towel.

'Is that all? God, Nora, you nearly frightened the life out of me! Look around you. You're the only woman on this beach wearing a top. You're the one who's odd, not me.'

'Well, I'm certainly not taking mine off. Just look at those middle-aged men over there eyeing all the young girls!'

'So what?' Tressy said tiredly. 'It isn't hurting anyone, is it?'

'It's disgusting!' Nora went muttering on, not reading her book any more but looking round the beach at everyone else. After half an hour she turned over and carefully oiled all her front, then lay down again. But within minutes she was sitting up. 'I was thinking about that sundress I want to wear on the boat tomorrow,' she remarked. 'If I took my top off I wouldn't get any strap marks, would I?'

Tressy opened one eye and looked at her. 'For God's sake, Nora, take it off. Let it all hang out.'

'Oh really! You're so vulgar.' But she took her top off and after nervously covering herself with her arms for a few minutes gradually exposed herself to what she thought was the avid gaze of every male over the age of twelve on the beach. Tressy grinned to herself and went back to sleep.

Nora had forgotten to oil her breasts. This fact became painfully apparent a couple of hours after they returned from the beach and she was dressing to go out after her bath. Tressy heard her give a yell of pain and went into her room to find her trying to put a bra on. The special oil had done its work well and the rest of her was a pale pink, but her breasts were fiery red. Tressy goggled and ran to the first aid cabinet, coming back to smear anti-burn cream on for her.

'You can't possibly put a bra on—it'll hurt too much. You'll have to go without one.'

Nora was shocked. 'I can't go without a bra!'

'Why not? I hardly ever wear one.'

Nora gave her a snooty look that spoke volumes. 'What will Mummy say?'

'Don't tell her. Honestly, Nora, you're unnatural, the way you tell your mother everything.'

So Nora went out for the first time in her life without a bra, and later spent a restless night unable to sleep. The next morning they were only a little better.

'What am I going to do?' she wailed, looking at herself in the mirror.

'Rub some more cream on and wear a loose sundress. No one's going to know, for heaven's sake.' Tressy was getting heartily fed up with Nora's complaining.

'Oh, and I so wanted everything to be perfect for today!'

Tressy ignored her; she was run off her feet blow-drying Nora's and her aunt's hair and doing their make-up before they left, and she hadn't even started to get ready herself. Cris had said he wanted to start at some ungodly hour and they were late already. She had only time to run upstairs to put on a pair of shorts and a loose top over a bikini, and brush her hair before Uncle Jack hooted impatiently on the car horn and it was time to go.

Michel had reserved a parking place for them near the quay and helped them to carry all the things Nora and her mother had insisted on bringing, not to mention the bottles of wine that Uncle Jack had brought along as his contribution to the day's outing.

Cris was on deck, waiting for them with another middle-aged English couple whom he introduced as Helen and Edward Young. He raised his eyebrows when he saw the amount of stuff the Sinclairs had brought with them and quickly crossed the gangplank to greet them and take a heavy portable video recorder and camera that Tressy was carrying for her uncle so that he could carry his precious wine.

'Which of this lot is yours?' he asked her.

'Oh, I travel light.' She gestured towards the sunglasses perched on top of her head. 'These are all I need.'

He looked at her in amazed disbelief. 'Then you're a woman in a million. A pearl beyond price.'

Tressy glanced frowningly up at him, expecting to find him mocking her as usual, but to her surprise saw that he was quite serious.

He smiled at her and, taking her hand, helped her across the gangplank. 'Welcome aboard the *Chimera*,' he said, and gave her a small wink that only she could see.

After a moment, Tressy smiled back at him and suddenly made up her mind that she was going to enjoy herself, that a day she hadn't particularly been looking forward to might turn out to be okay after all.

CHAPTER FIVE

AND it did turn out to be a good day, in so far as any day that included the close proximity of her aunt and uncle could be called good. But the presence on board of the other couple, the Youngs, helped a great deal, because the four older people tended to keep together, carefully sounding each other out by casual questions about holidays and houses, and establishing that their social and financial backgrounds were more or less equal. And once that was done they were able to relax and enjoy each other's company.

Tressy loved the boat. She sat alone on the deck up on the bow, as Cris took the boat out of the harbour, past the entrance with its twin lighthouse towers and out into the open sea. There were craft everywhere: motor cruisers like their own, sail-boats, pedalos, canoes, water-skiers being pulled along, big sightseeing boats, and even windsurfers quite a long way out, riding the swell. The wind caught at her hair and Tressy freed it from its restraining bach. She slipped off her sun-top and shorts and pushed them through an open window into a cabin behind her, then leant back, revelling in the breeze that cooled the warmth of the sun.

After they had cleared the beach area, Michel came forward carrying two glasses of champagne. Tressy looked at the one he gave her rather dubiously, remembering how squiffy she'd got on a mixture of wine and sun before, but thought, what the hell! and drank deeply. Michel was a good companion to have as they travelled westwards, parallel to the coastline and about half a mile away from it. Being a native, he was able to point out Cap Ferrat and the long Promenade des Anglais in Nice, the Upper Corniche high up in the hills, and then Antibes and Cannes, places that had only been names to her before. And he had anecdotes and stories to tell about every place.

'You love it here, don't you?' Tressy remarked, watching his animated face as he looked at the towns they passed.

'*Mais oui*. I could never leave the Riviera.'

'Do you live in Monte Carlo?'

'Yes, I have an apartment in the town.'

'And do you have a boat, too?'

He laughed. 'A boat, yes. But not one such as this. Only a sailing boat; what you call a yacht.'

They had finished their champagne some time ago, and now Michel stood up to get some more, but as he did so the boat lurched a bit and he had to grab the rail to keep his balance. Looking up, they saw that Cris was giving Nora a lesson in steering the boat; she waved to them, her face full of excitement, and the boat wobbled again.

Michel laughed. 'We go and join them, *oui*?'

Tressy was happy enough where she was, but thought she had better go and be sociable, so she went with him up to the bridge where Cris was standing beside Nora, ready to grab the wheel if need be. He had one hand casually on her shoulder and Nora had never looked so happy.

Turning to look at them, Cris smiled at Tressy and said, 'Perhaps you'd like to have a go too?' and Nora's face fell ludicrously.

Suddenly angry with them both, Tressy said shortly, 'No, thanks. Being able to handle a boat is hardly likely to be of much use to me back in London, now is it?'

His mouth thinning a little, Cris said to Michel, 'Take over here for me for a while, will you? I'll get another bottle of champagne out of the fridge.'

Michel took his place and Tressy moved to let Cris go past, but he put a firm hand in the small of her back and propelled her down into the cabin in front of him. 'What's got into you?' he demanded as soon as they were out of earshot in the galley.

'Nothing's got into me. I thought you came down here for more champagne,' she pointed out when he just stood and looked at her.

'So why did you jump down my throat just now?'

'Because I felt like it,' she retorted waspishly. 'Does there have to be a reason?'

'With anybody else, yes. But with you I'm beginning to have doubts. But you're right; you do seem to fly off the handle irrationally.'

'I'm not irrational,' she objected.

'Then you must have a reason,' he pointed out smoothly.

Cornered, Tressy burst out, 'Well, if you must know, I dislike seeing Nora making a fool of herself over you. *And* you encourage her.'

'Do I?' His left eyebrow rose questioningly.

'You know darn well you do. She's besotted about you!'

'But maybe I don't think she's making a fool of herself.'

Tressy looked at him suspiciously. 'You don't?'

'No. Maybe I like it.'

Her eyes widened incredulously. 'You're—you're serious about Nora?'

'Why? Do you find it so hard to believe?' he asked, his eyes on her face.

'Because I . . . I mean, that is, I don't of course . . .' But it was impossible to be either tactful or polite, not with this man, and she was suddenly angry again.

'Because you're all wrong for Nora! She isn't in your league at all.'

'Are you saying that I couldn't make her happy?'

Tressy was about to make a stinging retort, but then her breath caught in her throat; today Crispin was wearing just a pair of denim shorts, revealing the muscled body that she had already imagined. He was tanned and tall and very, very masculine. Slowly she said, 'I'm quite sure you could make any woman happy—if you wanted to.'

'And don't you think that, if she were my wife, I would want to make Nora happy?'

'Oh yes, for a time, but then you'd start to despise her because she was trying too hard to please you. And then you'd just be polite.'

'Really?' His tone was sneering, derisive. 'You know me so well?'

'*That's* exactly what I mean,' Tressy said hotly. 'You'd speak to Nora in that tone and you'd crush her. She isn't insensitive, you know.'

He gave her an odd kind of look. 'And you? If it were you, would you try to please me?'

'No, I damn well wouldn't!' she retorted vehemently.

Cris grinned and suddenly the whole conversation seemed ridiculous. 'That's what I thought. Here, take this up to the others, will you?' And taking some champagne from the fridge, he put the cold bottle into her arms, so that she nearly dropped it.

Afterwards, Tressy tried to work out whether he had been serious during that conversation or not, but he was such an enigma that she couldn't make up her mind. If he was, then it would make Nora ecstatically happy in the short term, but Tressy was still sure that they were fundamentally unsuited. So did she discourage her cousin or not? Eventually she resolved to just stay out of it and watch what happened.

But if Cris was serious about Nora he gave no particular sign of it, although he did spend quite a lot of time with her that day. But he also spent time with all his guests, and that included Tressy, sitting beside her when they anchored off St Tropez for lunch and coming to sit with her in her favourite place in the bow on their return journey while Michel took the wheel.

'You look two shades browner than you did this morning already,' he observed as he ran his eyes over her. 'Why isn't Nora sunbathing?'

'She can't,' Tressy answered without thinking. 'She burnt her boobs on the beach the other day and can't get her top on.'

Cris burst out laughing. 'I didn't think she was that daring!'

'Only because she hasn't had any encouragement to break out before.'

'Which you're providing now?'

'Do you disapprove?' she challenged.

He grinned and lay back beside her. 'Don't try to provoke me, woman, I'm not in the mood. Shut up and enjoy the sun.'

Tressy laughed too, and turned over on to her front so that she could look at him, studying his hard profile as he lay with his eyes closed. 'Why aren't you married already?' she asked after several minutes.

His lips curved. 'So you're becoming curious, are you?'

'Not in the least,' Tressy snapped, and got up and flounced away, the sound of his laughter making her angrier than ever.

It *had* been a good day; all the Sinclairs had enjoyed it, although Tressy had one or two reservations about Cris; she still didn't know whether he was serious about Nora or not, but decided to just let it ride and see what happened. Her aunt and uncle had got on well with the Youngs and the acquaintance soon blossomed into friendship, with the four of them seeing each other most days. And somehow Tressy found that she was reluctantly making up a foursome with Nora, Crispin and Michel and they, too, began to see each other nearly every day. Occasionally other people were invited along, but usually it worked out that just the four of them would go for a boat trip, or else by car to explore other towns along the coast, or inland to old villages perched like eagles' nests on the top of great, clifflike hills among the many gorges a few miles inland.

Tressy expected her aunt and uncle to be annoyed that she was invited along with Nora, but one day her aunt took her aside and, after giving her a rather involved lecture on the responsibility and gratitude she owed them and reminding her that her morals must be beyond reproach while she was with them, more or less said that it was okay for her to go so long as she stayed in the background and merely acted as a sort of chaperone for Nora. Which, Tressy realised with an inward laugh, didn't say much for her aunt's opinion of Cris and Michel's morals either. Or perhaps Aunt Grace believed that every man turned into a seducer given the slightest opportunity or encouragement.

Most foursomes naturally divide into two couples, and Tressy had expected this one to be the same, with her and Michel paired off together, but right from the start they had been just four people with no splitting into pairs, all constantly changing around like figures in a dance. And, although he didn't make it obvious, Tressy noticed that it was Cris who generally arranged this. She wondered if he wanted to give himself more time before committing himself to the relationship;

after all, he hadn't really known Nora all that long. And he certainly wasn't behaving in a very loverlike way. As a host he was perfect, but Tressy had never seen him do more than take Nora's arm to help her when she needed it or occasionally put a casual arm across her shoulders when they walked along together. But he did that with Tressy, too. Or tried to, because she usually moved away from him when he did, and she often tried to keep with Michel so that Cris could spend more time with Nora, but somehow she always found herself adroitly outmanoeuvred.

Nora, of course, was in seventh heaven. She was convinced that Cris really liked her and made a great fuss about her appearance and her clothes, seeming to feel that she must look well turned out and neat all the time. She never sat in the bow of the boat because it blew her hair about and her body turned only slowly brown, whereas Tressy soon had a beautiful golden tan. It was almost pathetic the way Nora put herself out to try to please Crispin, listening attentively to everything he said and always agreeing with his opinions and suggestions for their entertainment, even if it was something she knew she wasn't going to enjoy. She wasn't, for example, a terribly good sailor, but nothing on earth would have kept her away from the *Chimera* if Cris suggested a trip on it. And she seldom swam with them when they anchored in a bay somewhere along the coast, not because she couldn't swim, but because she didn't want to mess her hair up. Maybe she was right, maybe that was the kind of image Crispin wanted his future wife to have; Tressy didn't know, she only knew that she enjoyed herself much more when she didn't wear make-up and didn't care what her hair looked like. So perhaps she was displaying her lower class origins or something, but then she wasn't husband-chasing. And she wasn't afraid to get into an argument with Cris if she didn't agree with him, a fact that made Nora writhe in grim-faced silence until they were alone and she could have a go at Tressy, who took not the slightest notice.

Of them all, it was Michel who possibly got the most out of their outings. As a Frenchman, he picked up all the undercurrents and probably found them most amusing, but never made any remarks. And, although he knew plenty of people in the area, he seemed content to come along with them whenever Cris suggested it. Tressy wondered about Michel; he never seemed to do any work and never spoke of a career and, even though he came from a very old and aristocratic family, he didn't seem to have a great deal of money, leaving Crispin to pick up the bills nearly all the time. Perhaps he was some kind of modern gigolo, Tressy thought, intrigued. But if so why was he wasting his time on them? Nora was all too obviously gone on Cris, and Tressy hadn't any money. Only perhaps he didn't know that. The idea came as a surprise, but she supposed it could be possible that Michel had taken it for granted that because Nora was rich she was too. She grinned. It would be interesting to see how he reacted when she enlightened him.

The next day was the Friday of the Sinclairs' party. They had invited everyone they knew on the Riviera, which included quite a few people they had only met during the past couple of weeks. They had employed caterers and extra staff for the evening, but even so Aunt Grace managed to keep Tressy on her feet all day long, helping to prepare the guest rooms for people who were staying overnight, arranging flowers, passing instructions to her uncle, much to his annoyance, and often being kept busy just because her aunt couldn't bear to see her idle.

So she was late coming down and the party was well

into its second or third drink when she came down the long, curving staircase into the hall. Nora had been moved to be generous and had passed on a pale turquoise sleeveless silk shift that did nothing for her and which she imagined wouldn't do anything for Tressy either, otherwise she wouldn't have given it to her, but the colour was just right to complement Tressy's hair and show off her tan. It was a little too big for her, but the material looked better hanging in loose folds and she had fastened it with a wide gold belt round her slender waist. She wore high-heeled gold sandals to match and had put her hair up into a casual chignon from which little tendrils of hair escaped tantalisingly.

Nearly all of the guests were out in the garden or on the terrace. The trees had been hung with coloured lights and some old Chinese lanterns that they had found in a storeroom, and there were glass-protected candles poked in among the shrubs and flowers that gave a soft, pleasant glow to the atmosphere. Tressy paused by the French windows, looking out at the scene: the lights, the well-dressed guests, laughing and chatting as if lives depended upon it, everyone with a drink in their hand. She saw Crispin, in a dark dinner jacket this time, talking to the Youngs over by the pool, and wondered why Nora wasn't with him, until she saw her with Michel, being introduced to some friends he had brought with him. Tressy watched her cousin, her lips curled in genuine amusement; Nora was trying to be polite and interested, but it was obvious from the way she kept edging away from the group that she was dying to get back to claim Cris and to show him off to everyone there as her especial property.

'It's all right, Cinderella, you can come to the ball.'

Tressy looked quickly round and saw that Cris had

come up the steps and was holding out his hand to her. Her eyes swept back to Nora, only to see the other girl break free from her group and turn to hurry away, her face falling when she saw that Crispin had gone and becoming bleak when she saw where he had gone. Ignoring his hand, Tressy started to go down the steps. 'Cinderella,' she said coldly, 'had a ball dress and glass slippers.'

'And no doubt she looked almost as lovely as you do,' he agreed.

Tressy blinked. 'This dress is one of Nora's.'

'You swop clothes with each other?' He took a firm hold of her arm.

She laughed shortly. 'You're joking! Nora wouldn't be seen dead in anything of mine. No, this is one of her cast-offs,' she said with just a touch of bitterness.

'But you took it?'

'Of course. I'm used to wearing Nora's old clothes. They've been passed on to me ever since I was a child.'

He stopped and took a couple of glasses of champagne from a waiter and put one into her hand. 'So you're just a secondhand Rose.'

'Something like that,' she agreed frigidly.

Lifting his glass, Cris clinked it against hers. 'Stop trying to freeze me out. It won't work.'

Her eyes flew quickly up to his face. 'What do you mean?'

'I mean that nothing you say is going to shock me, so don't . . .' He broke off as Nora came up to them.

'Tressy, Mummy wants you.' Then she slipped her hand through Crispin's arm and said, 'Do come and meet these friends of ours who're staying in Cannes; they're dying to meet you.'

Cris gave Tressy a quick look to which she didn't respond, and then let himself be led away. Her aunt, of course, hadn't wanted her at all, so she talked to the people she knew and some others who introduced themselves until it was time to eat, and then Michel came to find her and took her into the dining-room where the buffet was laid out. The food was gorgeous, with no expense spared. Tressy had to admit that her aunt knew how to entertain; there was every delicacy one could imagine, including lots more of her best caviare.

She and Michel took their piled up plates out into the garden again and sat at one of the tables on the terrace.

'Are you enjoying the party?' she asked him.

'Of course, very much.' But he didn't sound particularly enthusiastic.

'I suppose you go to parties like this all the time?'

'Quite often,' he agreed, refilling her glass from a bottle of champagne that he'd stolen from a waiter.

Watching him closely, Tressy said, 'I've never been to a party like this before. You see, they don't usually ask the maid.'

He frowned. 'They have asked their maid?'

'I'm the maid,' she explained.

His eyebrows went up. 'But you are Leonora's cousin. Do I not have that right?'

'Yes, you do. But I don't have any money, you see, so Uncle Jack is paying me to be their maid and Nora's companion while they're here.'

To her surprise Michel only nodded. 'That is a very good arrangement. Very practical. We French are also very practical people. One of my aunts who lives in Paris, every year, she pays her godson to come and live in her house for the summer while he is on vacation from the Sorbonne and she comes to St Tropez for her holiday. It is good for both of them, you understand.'

Tressy looked at him rather impatiently. 'Doesn't it bother you that I'm poor, that I have no money *at all*?'

It was his turn to be surprised. 'No, why should it? We can't all be rich.'

'Are you? Are you rich, I mean?' she demanded bluntly.

He gave her a droll sort of sideways look that only a Frenchman can get away with without looking silly. 'Ah, I understand. You wish to know if I am a fortune-hunter, *n'est-ce pas*?' If he intended to embarrass her he didn't succeed; Tressy merely looked at him expectantly, so he smiled and said, 'No, I am not rich with money. My family had a great deal of money and estates once, but not now. So am I looking for a rich wife?' He shrugged eloquently. 'I admit that a rich wife would be very nice, but I am in no big hurry. I enjoy my life as it is, and I am lucky in that I have many friends. I am rich in my friends.'

'You mean you have rich friends like Cris to pick up the tab all the time,' Tressy translated crudely.

Michel looked affronted and opened his mouth to protest, but before he could say anything a hand descended on Tressy's shoulder, gripping hard.

Above her, Cris said, 'Let's dance, shall we?' But he gave her no time to think about it, pulling her up from her chair and propelling her on to the lawn where a few other couples were dancing. Then he put a firm arm round her waist and began to move in time with the music.

'Do you mind?' Tressy exclaimed indignantly. 'What right do you have to drag me away from Michel to dance with you?'

'And just what right do you think you have to be damn rude to Michel?' Cris hit back, his face grim. 'Just what the hell has it got to do with you whether I pick up the tabs or not?'

At his first burst of anger, Tressy had instinctively tried to free herself and walk away, but Crispin only held her more tightly, his arm holding her slender body firmly against him. 'I don't want to dance.' She tried in vain to push him away as they moved through the pale orange light thrown by a Chinese lantern.

'All right.' They were in a dark corner of the garden now and, without warning, he moved over to the gate leading down to the beach, and went through it, keeping a firm hold on her waist so that she had to go with him, down the path through the pine and olive trees, not stopping until they reached a wider spot with a view overlooking the sea.

Then he swung round on her and said angrily, 'Michel is a friend of mine, and it's nothing to do with you which of us pays the bills. That's strictly between him and me. If it comes to that,' he said brutally, 'I don't ever see you offering to pay.'

Tressy gasped and turned to go back up the path, but Cris caught her wrist and held on to it. 'Oh, no, you don't. You're not running out on this one. Why did you say that to Michel?'

As angry now as he was, Tressy snapped back, 'Because I wanted to know if he was a fortune-hunter, that's why. I'm supposed to be looking after Nora and . . .'

'Rubbish! You couldn't care less who Nora marries,' Cris told her roundly.

'Well, I'd certainly feel sorry for her if she married *you*,' Tressy retorted. 'And as for not paying my way—well, that's easily remedied; I just won't go out with you again. You don't seriously think I ever wanted to, do you?' She laughed jeeringly. 'Spending day after day with you and your toffee-nosed friend certainly isn't my idea of fun!'

'No? Then why come along?'

'Because I'm *paid* to,' Tressy told him triumphantly. 'Uncle Jack pays me to go with Nora and make sure you don't molest his precious daughter,' she taunted him.

'Really? Then what about his precious niece?' Too late, Tressy realised that she'd goaded him too far and tried to turn and run, but Crispin jerked her towards him and caught her in his arms. 'So I'll just have to molest you instead, won't I?' And before she could do anything to prevent him, his mouth was on hers, taking her lips with a fierce, angry passion.

Tressy made a convulsive movement to get away, but he put a hand in her hair and bent her backwards, holding her hard against him as he assaulted her mouth. She tried to beat at his chest, her hands balled into angry fists, but was pinned too tightly against him, and when she tried to move her head away he tightened his grip on her hair and hurt her. 'You pig!' She swore at him, but it only came out as a sound of fury against his mouth. He ignored her anger, trying to dominate her into submission, his lips forcefully persuasive.

But Tressy kept her mouth tightly shut, determined not to give in, hating him for his superior strength that could humble her so easily. Tears of fury came into her eyes as she fought to resist him, but his mouth moved insinuatingly against hers and there was a fleeting memory that threw her off guard. Her lips softened a little and Crispin was swift to take full advantage of her weakness, opening her mouth and kissing her with a yearning hunger that sent her senses reeling.

When at last he let her go, Tressy slowly opened her eyes and stared at him. 'It—it wasn't a dream,' she said on a long sigh of recognition.

Cris still had his hand in her hair and was looking

down at her langorous eyes, her sensuously parted mouth. 'What wasn't?' he asked softly.

'You *did* kiss me before. In my room the night you brought me home. I thought it was a dream—until now.' A thought occurred to her and she stiffened. 'Did—did anything else happen that I don't remember?'

Crispin laughed in delighted amusement. 'The temptation to lie just to see your face is almost irresistible,' he teased her. 'But no, my sweet, nothing else happened. Only this,' he added as his eyes darkened and he bent to kiss her again.

This time she put up only a token resistance, submitting to the importunities of his mouth until his hand moved to cover her breast. Then she broke free and stepped away from him, her eyes wide as she stood and stared at him, one arm held across her body as if to shield herself.

Cris frowned and didn't try to reach for her again. His had been only a hollow victory, and he knew it; although Tressy had submitted to his kiss, she hadn't responded or allowed him to caress her. Leaning against the wall that guarded the path from the steep fall to the rocky beach below, he took a packet of cigarettes from his pocket and lit one, drawing on it deeply. 'I hope you're going to apologise to Michel,' he said evenly, taking up the subject again as if nothing had happened in between.

Tressy gulped and tried to answer just as matter-of-factly. 'Maybe.' She, too, leant against the wall, but with her elbows on it, looking out to sea.

'There's no maybe about it; you'll do it,' he told her forcefully.

She gave a derisive laugh. 'Well, that sounds more like the Crispin Fox we all know and love!'

His free hand shot out and caught her arm, gripped

it hard, and for a moment she thought he was going to kiss her again, but when she flinched away he let her go, leaving red marks on her bare arm. After a moment, he said, 'Why don't we call a truce and promise not to provoke each other?'

'It wouldn't last,' Tressy answered with certainty.

'Not even for tonight?'

She turned, her head on a level with his and found him watching her intently. The memory of those kisses came back and she quickly looked away, letting her hair fall forward to screen her face.

'Very useful,' Crispin remarked. 'Ostriches do that as well.'

'Do what?' she asked, startled.

'Hide their heads in the sand.'

Tressy tossed her hair back, her eyes flashing in angry defiance. 'Go to hell!' she told him.

'Very possibly,' he said dryly. 'And in the meantime, are you going to continue to chaperone Nora and earn the wages your uncle's paying you?'

She shrugged. 'I don't have any choice, I suppose.'

Cris laughed harshly, 'Nicely put!'

Her eyes grew angry again. 'But I don't have to take anything from you. I'll pay my own way in future.'

He contemplated her dispassionately for a few moments, then said, much to her relief, 'When I invite you out you are my guest just as much as Nora and Michel—and I don't allow my guests to pay, whether they happen to be male or female. Understood?'

'Sure, if that's the way you want it.' Tressy wanted to go back to the party but somehow couldn't bring herself to just walk away, so instead she looked to her left across the bay to Menton with its floodlit Cathedral set high on a hill and the houses and narrow streets of the old town clustered around it. And below, on the shoreline where a long arm of the harbour wall ended in a small lighthouse, there was a glistening necklace of lights reflected in the still sea. The moon, too, was out, giving a soft, chocolate-box atmosphere to the scene. The French Riviera by moonlight, she mused—what better place for romance? Only the way that Cris had kissed her hadn't been romantic, not in the least. She turned abruptly. 'I'm going back.'

'All right.' He tossed his cigarette end over the wall and turned to follow her, the scent of the pine trees sharp in the night air.

They had gone further than she realised and it took them several minutes to climb back up the steep path. The small group of musicians that Uncle Jack had hired for the evening were taking a break as they reached the garden and there was nothing to distract the curious eyes that watched them. And Cris didn't help matters by placing an arm round her waist as they walked across the lawn. Tressy tried to move away, but he kept her firmly by his side. She looked round, hoping that Nora wasn't anywhere near, but her cousin came out on to the terrace, obviously searching for Crispin, her face falling when she saw them together.

Tressy tried to retrieve the situation as much as she could by lifting her hand to wave and calling out, 'Hi, we've been looking for you. Where were you?'

Nora came over, eyeing them uncertainly. 'I was inside. Did you want me?' she added hopefully, looking at Cris.

'Cris has something to ask you, haven't you, Cris?'

'Why, yes.' Fortunately he followed her lead. 'I was wondering if you would care to spend the day in Menton tomorrow? The four of us, of course,' he added when Nora hesitated.

The disappointment in Nora's eyes was plain to see, and Tressy felt a flash of anger at her inability to conceal her feelings. 'Excuse me,' she said abruptly, and strode away, leaving them together, but when the band returned she noticed that Cris danced with someone else before he danced with Nora.

Tressy sat on the terrace wall, looking out over the lawn, her eyes drawn to the couple as they moved slowly in time to the music. He held Nora loosely, his head a little to one side as he listened to her talking animatedly, gesturing with her free hand. He was quite the tallest and best-looking man there, his tan deeper now, his lithe body moving easily, attracting the glances of every woman at the party. There was something about him that drew women's eyes, an arrant masculinity that they instinctively recognised and which excited their imaginations, arousing their primitive instinct to be mastered, perhaps. But Crispin's powerful maleness was contained beneath several layers of civilised good manners and it would, Tressy guessed, take a great deal of provocation to pierce his self-containment. She sensed that although he was listening to Nora, he wasn't giving her his full attention, but he was much too polite to show it, to be unkind to a woman in any way. Except to her. He had been downright rude to her on more than one occasion, Tressy remembered indignantly.

As if there was telepathy between them, Cris chose that moment to look up, his eyes meeting hers and holding them locked to his. It was really too far away to be sure, but she felt a distinct challenge in his gaze and her chin came up in immediate defiance. Almost she could feel his kisses again on her lips, the fierce strength of his hands as he had held her prisoner in his embrace. She flushed as she realised that he had intended her to remember and her eyes flashed angrily, but she didn't look away, refusing to give him the satisfaction of disconcerting her. Who would have won in the end she never knew, because Nora, wondering why he had slowed down, pulled him round so that all Tressy could see was his back.

For the rest of the evening she kept out of his way, which was easy, because Cris made no attempt to come near her again, although Michel later came up and asked her to dance. Tressy looked at him rather guiltily. 'Are you sure you want to?'

'But of course. Why should I not wish to dance with you?' he asked as he put his arm round her waist.

'I was very rude to you earlier on.'

He shrugged expansively. 'One can forgive a beautiful woman anything.'

'Oh, for heaven's sake! How can you say that? The way someone looks can't excuse what they do,' Tressy exclaimed. 'You surely don't believe it?'

Michel looked amused. 'If I don't, then I should be angry with you, *hein*?'

'Well, so you should,' Tressy admitted. She hesitated. 'Cris says I have to apologise to you.'

His eyebrows rose. 'And are you going to obey him?'

'Certainly not! He can't order *me* around. Although,' she added after a moment, 'if he hadn't ordered me to I might have said I was sorry.'

The Frenchman laughed delightedly. 'So, honour is satisfied. And I forgive you, but not because you are a beautiful woman.' He shook his head. 'You English—I shall never fully understand you, I think.'

The music changed to a fast beat number and the party began to really liven up. Tressy danced with everyone who asked her and let herself go with the music, getting as hot and breathless as all the other dancers. But she felt a strange detachment, as if only half of her was taking part, and when, inevitably, people started getting drunk enough to jump in the pool, some not even bothering to change into swimsuits, Tressy went inside and sat in an armchair in the deserted and unlit drawing-room, kicking off her sandals and tucking her feet under her. Through the open windows she could hear the shouts of encouragement and high-pitched squeaks as a girl got thrown in. Nora was out there; Tressy recognised her laugh, but it didn't sound as if she'd gone in the water yet, and she would probably make sure she didn't unless Crispin went in too, and somehow Tressy couldn't envisage him doing so, not at a party.

And she was right; twenty minutes or so later she heard his voice in the hall, saying goodnight to some departing guests, and Nora's voice, too, joined in the chorus of goodbyes. Then Cris said, 'I expect you'll be tired in the morning so we won't come to pick you up until ten-thirty. Will that be okay?'

'Yes, of course.' Tressy heard Nora hesitate. 'Crispin, I wondered if we could have a round of golf some time. Daddy's been teaching me and I'm quite good. I . . .'

'What a good idea! We'll have to arrange a day. Tressy does play, doesn't she? I know Michel does.'

'Oh, but I . . .'

'Where is Tressy, by the way? I haven't said goodnight to her.'

'I don't know.' Nora sounded sulky. 'I expect she's gone to bed. Cris, I . . .'

He laughed easily. 'You're not going to shorten my name as well, are you?'

'Oh *no*. I *like* Crispin,' she said fervently.

'Thank you. See you tomorrow, then. You'll tell Tressy the time, won't you? And thank you again for a very pleasant evening.'

Tressy heard the door shut behind him and then kept very quiet until Nora's footsteps went past and she could go safely up to bed.

CHAPTER SIX

THE day at Menton somehow got out of hand. It started off no differently from any other day; Cris picked them up at ten-thirty and they drove down to the harbour, where Michel had the boat all ready to go. Nora had stayed up until the end of the party and was tired, but was being over-bright to try to hide it, sitting in the front of the car next to Cris and determined to hold his attention, while Tressy lolled in the back with her feet up on the seat, hoping it would annoy him; but it only annoyed Nora. As they reached the harbour she turned round and exclaimed, 'Tressy! You'll ruin the upholstery. Take your feet off at once!'

'So, he can afford to buy a new one, can't he?' Tressy retorted as she got out. She turned to Crispin. 'Why don't you get yourself an interesting car?'

'You don't think a Rolls is interesting?'

'Good heavens, no!' She made a disdainful gesture. 'They're two a penny in Monte Carlo.'

'What, then, would you suggest?' He went round to take Nora's bags from the boot.

'Why don't you get a sports car—a Ferrari or a Maserati? Something with some real power in the engine.'

'A Rolls is pretty powerful.'

'But you never drive it fast.'

'There does happen to be a speed limit on French roads, or hadn't you noticed?' He grinned and put a hand on her shoulder as they walked towards the boat. 'I should have known you were a speed merchant.'

'But not,' Tressy replied coolly, trying to move away, 'a fast lady.'

But he only gave a rich masculine laugh of genuine amusement and didn't let go her shoulder until he helped her, quite unnecessarily, across the gangplank.

It was only a short distance by sea from Monte Carlo to Menton, passing the promontory of Cap Martin where Tressy could just make out the villa nestling among the trees. Once they were clear of all the vessels around the harbour, Cris handed over the wheel to Michel and came to join her in her usual place on the bow, his long frame stretched alongside her.

'Why do you always sit up here?' he asked.

'I don't know. I like the breeze, I guess.'

'Or is it because Nora has ordered you to keep out of the way?' he demanded roughly.

'Why no, of course not.' She turned to quickly deny it just as the boat hit the wash of another vessel and she was thrown against him, her shoulder touching his bare chest. He immediately put his arms round her to steady her, and her heart gave a crazy kind of jump.

The boat got back on its usual even keel, but he didn't let her go. Instead his arms tightened and he said thickly, 'Tressy . . .'

Looking up, she saw the dark fire in his eyes and quickly pulled free, turning so that her back was towards him. 'I come up here because I like to be alone,' she snapped.

'Of course—I should have remembered how boring you find our company.' But he didn't sound at all put out. Lifting his hand, he began to trace the line of her spine with a long finger, over her bikini strap and on down.

Tressy found she couldn't stand it and hastily turned on to her knees, facing him. 'Don't do that!'

'Why not?' He was watching her with a strange look in his eyes, partly amused but something else she couldn't fathom.

'Because I don't like it, of course. That's why not.'

'Don't you? Or is it that you're not as immune to me as you like to think you are?' he asked softly.

Her heart began to thump again, but she answered coldly, 'You don't turn me on, if that's what you mean.'

'No? Then why be in such a hurry to move away?'

'Because I don't like being—touched.'

His lids were half closed against the sun so she couldn't read his reaction, but he merely said lazily, 'What a rag-bag of emotions you are! Somebody ought to give you a good shake to get everything back into perspective again. What have you got against men, anyway?'

'What makes you think I have?' She relaxed a little and sat back as he made no further move to touch her.

'It stands out a mile. Somewhere along the line you've been hurt, and you're building a wall around yourself that has "Keep Out" signs all over it.'

'So why don't you read the signs?'

He grinned. 'Oh, I could never resist a challenge.'

Tressy could willingly have hit him. Blue eyes flashing, she said with bitter anger, 'You like playing games with people, don't you? You find it amusing to be the puppet-master and to manipulate people. But you needn't think you can use me as a pawn, because I . . .' She broke off as Cris suddenly sat up and caught hold of her arms, gripping tightly.

'I am *not* playing any kind of a game,' he told her forcefully. 'Especially not with you.'

He went on to say something else, but his words were lost as the hooter just above their heads sounded its imperious warning. Tressy nearly jumped out of

her skin and Cris looked quickly round to see that a
sailing dinghy was in difficulties just ahead of them,
its mast trailing in the sea. He ran aft to take over the
wheel and they stopped until they'd made sure that
everything was okay before going on again. They were
almost at Menton harbour now, so Crispin stayed at
the helm until they were safely moored.

Menton was at least a hundred years behind its
more prosperous neighbour but was very picturesque,
retaining its narrow cobbled streets between high old
buildings that climbed up the steep sides of a hill on
which perched the cathedral with its ornate, pink-
stone tower. There were square doorways surrounded
by tubs and hanging baskets of flowers, and
mysterious little alleyways with flights of steps that
disappeared into dark shadows. There was a peace and
sense of antiquity that was completely remote from the
modern brashness and hurry of Monte Carlo.

They had a drink in a café on the waterfront before
setting out to explore, strolling through the market
where colourful fruit and vegetable stalls were next to
slabs where the eyes of fish, of a sort you had never
imagined could exist, stared at you as you passed. The
four of them strolled on, stopping now and again to
look at the view as they climbed the branching double
staircase to the Cathedral square.

'They hold concerts out here now and again,' Cris
remarked. 'We'll have to come to one.'

'Oh, yes, please!' Nora enthused. Then she caught
sight of a sign over an open doorway. 'Look, a craft
shop. Let's go inside.' She glanced at Cris as if asking
permission and he nodded and moved to follow her.

Tressy didn't bother to go in; it wasn't that she
disliked such shops, but Nora was always going into
them, and you could have too much of a good thing,
especially when you could never afford to buy

anything. So she wandered over to look at the view of rich red and orange pantiled roofs below her and then, irresistibly drawn, began to wander up one of the narrow alleyways. After a couple of minutes Crispin joined her and pointed out a wooden balcony attached high up on the wall of one of the houses like a house-martin's nest.

'There's quite an interesting cemetery at the top of the hill here,' he told her, and led her round the corner into another alley.

Tressy hesitated for a moment. 'Where's Nora?'

'She's buying something; they'll catch us up,' Cris assured her, so she went with him.

The cemetery was shaded by dark cypress trees and seemed to be perched right on the edge of the hill behind the old town.

'Good heavens!' she exclaimed. 'I hope they don't have any landslides here, or you might find your dead relation back in the house with you!'

Cris shook with laughter. 'What a ghastly thought!' He drew her over to a wooden seat set in the shade of a thick tree and they sat down. 'Don't you find cemeteries depressing?'

'Not particularly.' Tressy shook her head. 'Not when the sun is shining. There's a very old one quite near where we live in London. It's been full up for years and is terribly overgrown, so it's full of birds and butterflies in the summer.'

'And you go there often?'

'Sometimes. When the house gets too clau-strophobic.'

'Are you from a large family?' he asked.

'No, there's just my mother and me.'

'Is your father dead?'

'I don't . . .' She stopped, realising where his questions were heading. 'Where are the others?' She stood up and would have moved away, but he caught her hand.

'They'll find us. Sit down in the shade again.' Slowly she obeyed him, but he didn't let go of her hand, looking down at it as if he found it absorbing. 'What would you like to do this afternoon? There's a windsurfing school here. You haven't tried that yet, have you?'

'No, but I'd like to,' she said enthusiastically, forgetting for the moment where her hand lay. 'But what about Nora? She might not be very keen.'

'But you want to, so we'll do it.' And turning her hand, he bent his head to kiss her palm.

Tressy stared at him, lips parted in surprise, so he leant forward and kissed them, too—a gentle, undemanding kiss that lasted only a few seconds. But it was enough to make her move away nervously. 'Nora will be looking for us.'

They walked back the way they'd come, but there was no sign of the others. 'Perhaps they've gone back to the boat,' said Tressy.

'I doubt it.' Cris shook his head. 'We must have missed them somewhere.' He glanced at his watch. 'It's almost one. I suggest we find somewhere to have some lunch.'

'We ought to find them,' Tressy insisted.

'Why?' His voice was taunting. 'What are you afraid of? That you're not chaperoning Nora—or that she isn't here to chaperone you?'

Her chin came up. 'I don't *need* a chaperone!'

'Good. Then let's go and eat.'

They found a restaurant near the beach where they sat outside under a large parasol and ate bouillabaisse, which Tressy had never had before and Cris insisted she try.

'Do you like it?' he asked.

'Mmm, it's delicious. It's all different kinds of fish, isn't it?'

'That's right. It's a speciality of the Mediterranean region.' He poured wine into their glasses and lifted his in a silent toast, but his eyes had that strange look again.

The food and the wine were good and the sun was hot on her back through the thin material of her sundress, but Tressy couldn't relax. He was sitting opposite her, but it was a small table and he was too close. Sometimes their bare legs touched under the table or their hands would brush. And she hadn't expected to be alone with him like this. She tried to keep her voice steady and to listen attentively when he talked, but she found herself forgetting to eat and her eyes strayed to his mouth and the clean-cut line of his jaw. He had very strong shoulders and his tan was much darker than hers, his skin a deep glistening brown. There weren't any hairs on the flat planes of his chest, and she was glad, she didn't like hairy men. His arms were hard and muscular, belying the sensitiveness of his hands.

She became aware that he was no longer speaking and slowly looked up. As she feared, he had caught her out, his mouth twisting in amusement as she flushed. Putting out his hand, he covered hers as it lay on the table. 'Come on,' he said softly.

After paying the bill, he led her across to the nearby private beach where he hired a couple of wooden loungers with thick mattresses, positioning them close together. Tressy stepped out of her sandals and pulled her sundress over her head, then put up her hands to lift the weight of hair off the back of her neck, twisting it into a plait which she tied with a ribbon.

Crispin drew in his breath sharply and she turned to see him looking at her with desire in his dark eyes. 'You're—perfect,' he said on a harsh, rasping note.

Quickly she lay down on her front on the lounger. 'I thought we were going windsurfing?'

'Better rest for a while after our meal first.' Taking off his sweat shirt and shorts, he stretched out next to her. 'Aren't you rather overdressed?' he remarked.

Two strips of bikini was hardly overdressed, but Tressy knew what he meant; every other woman on their stretch of beach, without exception, was topless.

She didn't answer or look round and he leaned towards her and said softly, 'Take it off.'

'No!'

'Are you afraid?'

Tressy turned her head to look at him, her eyes vulnerable and pleading. 'Yes,' she admitted at last, her voice little more than a whisper.

His face didn't change and his eyes stayed on hers, but he reached out and undid the clasp of her top, then gently pushed the material off her back, his fingers hotter than the sun, and drew it from under her. 'Turn over,' he commanded firmly.

For a moment her hands gripped the sides of the lounger, but then she slowly turned on to her side, facing him. His eyes devoured her, taking in each detail of her softly rising chest, the swell of her young, firm breasts, wakened now by tension. He put out a hand and she thought that he was going to touch her there, but he let it rest on her waist, gripping hard. 'You're lovely,' he said thickly. 'Exquisitely lovely.' Then, abruptly, he let her go and turned on to his front, turning his head away from her.

Tressy lay on her back, her pulses racing. She was attractive to men, she knew that, her auburn hair and slender figure making a stunning impact, and she had often seen desire in a man's eyes, but it had never affected her like this before. When a man wanted her he was in her power and she used him, and when he realised what she was doing and wanted her body in return, she dropped him; it was as simple as that. She didn't believe that there could ever be platonic friendship between men and women because no man she had ever been out with had not made a pass, sooner rather than later. Not that she knew many men with whom she could have been just friendly; her mother had sent her to an all-girls school, and the few members of the opposite sex that she had met while taking her hairdressing and beautician's course had nearly all been more interested in themselves or other men rather than girls. And the men she had met since then had only been interested in one thing, just as her mother had said they would. So she had used those she could and avoided the few that she had sensed wouldn't allow themselves to be used, and remained invulnerable to them all—until now. Now her pulses raced and her heart beat faster, and her body overheated, but not from the sun, even though she tried to convince herself that was the reason. That, and the wine they had drunk at lunchtime.

Her emotions gradually returned to normal as Tressy warned herself not to be stupid. Such feelings could be dangerous, could weaken her resistance. Cris was no different from other men, they all took advantage of the least weakness. And there was no point in making something out of this that wasn't there. So he turned her on. So what? Nothing would ever come of it. Cris was the type who only married rich girls like Nora or upper class girls who'd been to Benenden or Roedean and whose family knew his. Her type of girl might attract him into making her his mistress for a while, but then he'd leave her and go away, just as her father had walked out on her mother. And she wouldn't be used, she wouldn't! She wouldn't ever hear her mother say, 'I told you so.'

The wine and heat had a soporific effect, her eyelids fluttered and Tressy fell asleep, not waking until a shadow blotted out the sun. Languorously she opened her eyes and saw that Cris was sitting on his lounger facing her, his eyes leisurely examining her near-naked body. Tressy watched him, waiting until he reached her face and ready to make a nasty remark about voyeurism, but somehow, when their eyes met, the words died in her throat. Perhaps because there was no lechery in the way he looked at her, rather a strange tenderness; only strange because she wasn't used to seeing that emotion when men looked at her so openly.

'Hallo, sleepyhead.' He reached out and took her hand.

'Have I been asleep long?' she asked.

'Almost an hour. I was beginning to be afraid you'd burn,' he remarked, his eyes going again to her breasts.

'I think I have a deep enough tan now not to burn.'

'I could always apply some oil if it would help,' he offered with a look that this time was decidedly sexual.

Tressy sat up on the lounger and brought her knees up to her chin, so that most of her body was hidden from him. 'Are we going to try windsurfing now?' she asked, her voice a little unsteady.

He gave a low laugh and got to his feet, pulling her up with him. 'Of course, right now.'

There wasn't much space in between the loungers, and Tressy rocked unsteadily, automatically reaching out to grab something to stop herself overbalancing—and the only thing to grab was Cris. For a moment their bodies touched and a searing flame of heat seemed to ignite her already hot skin. Quickly she moved so that she wasn't touching him, but he had hold of her arms and she saw that he was looking down at her. Her eyes followed his and a flush of crimson stained her cheeks as she saw that her nipples had hardened and were standing proud of her breasts.

'So you're not so immune to me after all,' Cris murmured, unable to take his eyes away.

'Oh, for heaven's sake!' She wrenched herself free and sprang away from him. 'Are we going, or not?'

The windsurfing school was close by and they walked along the beach to it, wading through the shallows because it was easier on the feet than the pebbly beach. Cris hired a couple of windsurfers but dispensed with the services of a teacher, saying that he would show her how to use it himself. It was great fun once you got the hang of it, but until she did Tressy spent most of her time falling into the water, but Cris was always there to hoist her back up again and she realised why he hadn't wanted a teacher to do that job for him. After an hour or so she managed to keep her balance better and thoroughly enjoyed skimming over the wave tops behind Cris, turning the big sail to catch the breeze. But it was hard work for her arm and leg muscles and, although she protested, Tressy was quite glad when Cris insisted that she'd had enough for the first day.

While he took the surfers back, Tressy swam out to a raft anchored in the middle of the bay. It was about as far as she could comfortably manage, but her arms were tired and she had to catch hold of one of the loops of rope on the side of the raft and rest when she reached it, before pulling herself out of the sea. There was a ripple of water and Cris's head surfaced beside her.

'Are you okay?'

She nodded. 'Just resting for a minute.'

'Good girl!' He leant forward and kissed her lightly, his lips cold and wet against hers.

Tressy shook her head so that drops of water

splashed on to him. 'I feel like a mermaid,' she laughed.

Cris put his free arm round her waist and drew her to him so that their legs entwined. 'I'm glad you're not,' he told her, his eyes smiling wickedly down into hers. 'A tail could be most frustrating!'

It was getting late into the afternoon and most people were drifting back to their cars or hotels, so they had the raft to themselves. Cris hoisted her up and they sat in silent companionship for a while, watching the activity on the shore, the sun warm on their backs. When Cris put his arm round her, Tressy stiffened for a moment and then slowly relaxed, telling herself that it was merely casual, but it wasn't, because presently he began to gently stroke her back, his fingers causing delicious sensations that sent shivers down her spine. She knew she ought to tell him to stop or to get up and swim back to the beach, that to let him touch her was crazy, but she did neither of those things, just closed her eyes and let him go on.

His hands explored and caressed at the same time, from her neck right down her spine to her bikini and back again, taking interesting digressions to her waist and armpits and along the slender line of her shoulders. Cris was sitting a little behind her so that she couldn't see him without turning her head, and she kept her face averted, almost afraid to look at him. Lifting her rope of wet hair aside, he began to stroke her neck, his fingers scorching her skin, making her body feel hot in places nowhere near her neck. Then she gave an involuntary gasp as she felt his lips, featherlight, on her shoulder, moving towards the nape of her neck. She tried to move away then, but he put his hands on her trembling arms and said softly in her ear, 'Be still, my darling.' And went on kissing her, his lips and tongue tracing the long column of her neck and finding her earlobe, playing with it delicately until Tressy couldn't stand it any longer and she swung round to face him, her heart beating crazily, her eyes pleading with him to stop—to go on; she didn't even know herself.

His hands were still on her shoulders and they tightened as Cris looked into her face, his own eyes lit by a flame deep in their dark depths. 'Tressy.' He said her name in a thick, uneven voice and leaned forward to kiss her, but Tressy jerked her head away, then turned and dived into the water, making for the beach as fast as she could. There was a splash behind her and within a minute Cris was alongside, restricting his speed to match her own.

As Tressy waded ashore she was greeted by Nora's angry voice. 'So there you are! We've been looking for you everywhere.' Then, seeing that Tressy was topless, 'Must you *flaunt* yourself?'

But Michel looked his fill in open admiration and gallantly kissed her hand. '*Charmante!*'

Nora turned to Cris, trying to hide her anger. 'Whatever happened to you two? Once we got split up, we expected you to go back to the boat, so we went there to wait for you.'

Her voice was trembling and she was staring at Cris. Tressy followed her gaze and saw what Nora saw: a tall, good-looking man with a beautiful body, his wet trunks hiding nothing but the visual fact of his masculinity. Going up to Cris, Nora slipped her arm through his. 'Such a shame we got split up—we could have had a super day. I hope you weren't too bored—or embarrassed.' She began to walk along with him and her voice drifted back. 'Just because people do something in France that we don't do at home, it doesn't mean that one should lower one's standards and do the same thing. Don't you agree?

Why, some of the things they do here are hardly decent!'

Tressy almost laughed aloud; the only reason Nora was so dead against topless women was because her breasts had peeled where they'd got burnt and looked unsightly. If not, and she'd thought it would attract Cris, she'd have shed her top like a shot.

At the private beach, Tressy and then Cris showered off the sea salt and used the hired towels to dry themselves off, while the others stood by, waiting, Tressy put on her bikini top and a skirt, but undid her hair and let it spread loose on her shoulders to dry. Then they went to a nearby café for a drink and ice-creams. Nora refused at first, but Michel teased her and Cris encouraged her so that she gave in and was soon enjoying a bowl filled with four different flavours of ice-cream with fresh piped cream and nuts on the top.

'What would you like to do this evening?' Cris asked them. Negligently he reached an arm along the back of Tressy's chair and began to play with a lock of her hair, twining it round his fingers. 'There's a casino here, and I thought it might be fun to have a meal somewhere and then go on to the casino and sail back to Monte by night. The lights along the coast are quite spectacular from the sea.'

He was looking towards Tressy as he finished speaking, but she stayed silent and let Nora say eagerly, 'That sounds a super idea! I'd love to.' Her face fell. 'But I didn't bring a dress to wear.'

'Well, that's easily remedied. The shops are still open.'

They found a clothes shop nearby and Cris bought them each a dress; Nora choosing a midnight-blue tight-skirted number with a strapless top which she obviously thought made her look very sophisticated.

She paraded before the men in it, her excitement high, while Tressy looked through the racks and chose a simple white dress with a halter neck and a skirt that gathered on the hips, falling into soft swathes down to her mid-calves. She tried it on in the fitting-room and then took it off again, letting Nora have the limelight, feeling rather guilty at having deserted her all day. There was no price tag on the dress—Tressy looked— but the shop smelt expensive and for a moment she hesitated, then shrugged; what the hell, Cris wouldn't have offered to buy them if he couldn't afford it.

Cris raised his eyebrows when she came out of the fitting-room in her ordinary clothes. 'Don't you like it?'

'Yes, thanks, it's fine.'

'But you don't intend to give us a preview?' He looked amused when she shook her head. 'You'll need shoes to match, won't you?'

The assistant brought them several pairs to try, and Tressy settled for plain white high-heeled sandals while Nora picked a mixture of gold and silver. Then Michel tactfully took them to wait outside while Cris settled the bill. When he rejoined them he quite deliberately came over to Tressy and put his arm round her waist as they walked back to the boat.

After a few minutes she couldn't resist asking, 'How much did they cost, these clothes?'

'There are some questions,' he replied with laughter in his voice, 'that nice girls don't ask.'

'But I'd like to know.'

'Why?'

'Because I'm not sure I want to accept presents from you.'

'Nora doesn't seem to mind,' he pointed out mildly.

'It's different for Nora.'

'Is it? I don't see why.'

Tressy began to think that he was being deliberately obtuse. 'Nora can afford to buy anything she wants; I can't. You know that.'

His fingers tightened on her waist. 'Are you saying that buying you a dress is charity?' he demanded, his voice changing.

'Well, isn't it?'

'No, it damn well isn't! Why can't you accept it in the spirit that it was meant? I was merely providing you both with something suitable to wear so that we could go to the Casino tonight. And I had no other motives, whatever that warped brain of yours is thinking.'

Indignantly, Tressy stopped and faced him. 'All right, if that's what you want me to believe. But it would have been a darn sight cheaper to have taken us home to change and gone to the Casino in Monte,' she added tartly.

Angry now, Cris said forcefully, 'How I spend my money is my affair. And if I want to buy you presents I shall go ahead and do it.'

Her cheeks flushed. 'But I don't have to accept them!'

Cris opened his mouth to make a biting retort and Tressy was quite ready to throw the box containing her dress back at him, but both of them realised that Nora and Michel were coming up close behind them, aware that they were rowing and their eyes full of curiosity. So Cris put a hand firmly under her elbow and made her walk with him again.

When they got back to the *Chimera* they all went to different cabins to change, but as Tressy went to go into hers, Cris stopped her in the doorway. 'I also got these for you,' he said harshly, taking a small bag from his pocket and thrusting it into her hand. 'But perhaps you'll be more inclined to accept them if I said that I

bought them so that I could put them on you myself!'
And then he strode past her and went into his own
cabin.

Mystified, Tressy went inside and shut the door,
then opened the bag and took out a handful of delicate
white lace and silk that turned out to be the most
exquisite pair of panties she had ever seen, so fine that
even her delighted breath blew them like a butterfly
flapping its wings. How could she ever wear them?
They were much too beautiful, even more delicate
than the ones Nora had shown her before their
holiday. Bright spots of colour came to her cheeks as
she remembered Cris's gibe about wanting to put
them on her himself. Well, at least he hadn't said take
them off! And he wouldn't have said anything at all if
she hadn't made him angry. For a moment she
wondered what it would be like to have Cris undress
her, his hands caressing her as they had on the raft,
but then she heard Nora moving around in the next
door cabin and wondered if her cousin, too, had the
same erotic thoughts.

She wore the panties; no woman in her right mind
could have resisted them, and the white dress was
perfect against her deep golden tan. Usually she
dressed quickly, but this evening she took her time,
using the hair dryer she found in the cabin to blow-
dry her hair into an almost Grecian style that went
well with the dress, and she had enough make-up in
her bag to do a fairly professional job on her face. Any
minute Tressy expected Nora to summon her to do
her hair and face as well, and she was surprised when
she heard the next cabin's door close behind Nora as
she went up on deck. Tressy went up about ten
minutes later and found them all having pre-dinner
drinks, Nora in her new dress and the men in white
tuxedos.

Cris was half-leaning on the rail, laughing at something Michel was saying, but the laugh died and an arrested expression came into his eyes as he saw her standing in the doorway. Slowly he straightened up, put down his drink and came towards her, his eyes never leaving her face. Taking her hand in both of his, he raised it to his lips and kissed it lingeringly. Tressy gazed at him, her heart giving that crazy jerk again as she saw the warmth in his eyes. And suddenly the world seemed to have narrowed down to the small circle in which they stood and she was aware of nothing but Cris's nearness and the touch of his hand. The future, too, seemed somehow to be a part of the circle, all her hopes and ambitions, everything that she could want or expect from life seemed to be possible now, and she gave a long sigh of wonder. Slowly she lifted her free hand and placed it over his.

'But you are *très belle* tonight, *ma chérie. Ravissante!*'

Michel's voice broke their charmed circle and Tressy turned to smile at the other man, cheeks flushed, her eyes like diamonds. 'Thank you. You look pretty good yourself.'

He laughed. 'A Frenchwoman would never say that.' He drew her down beside him and Cris handed her a drink, smiling down at her before going to sit opposite, next to Nora. Tressy looked at her cousin and saw that she was, for once, sitting still and quiet, gazing down at her drink, answering only in monosyllables when anyone spoke to her. And she remained subdued throughout the evening, at the restaurant where they dined in the open air to the music of an accordionist playing traditional folk songs of Provence, and later in the completely opposite, sophisticated atmosphere of the Casino with its plush décor and gaming tables.

It occurred to Tressy that Nora might be sulking, but she pushed the thought aside; life was suddenly full of possibilities and it was heady stuff. Cris stayed by her side all evening, often putting what seemed like a proprietorial arm round her waist, making it plain that he wanted to be with her. And when they sailed the boat back to Monte Carlo and she would have gone to her usual place at the bow, he said assertively, 'Stay with me,' and after only a moment's hesitation she joined him at the wheel, letting him put his arm round her shoulders as he steered them through the soft night, made magical by the thousands of reflected lights from the shore.

It was in the early hours before they got back to the villa. Cris drove them home and this time it was Tressy who sat beside him. At the door he took her hand to say goodnight and kissed her lightly on both cheeks in the French manner, although the pressure of his hand told her that if the others hadn't been there he would have kissed her properly. But Nora stood resolutely waiting so that they went inside together and as soon as the door was shut went upstairs without even saying good night.

The Sinclairs all had lunch together at home the next day, and Nora was again very quiet, although no one took much notice because she was always quieter at home; she had once read that men liked animated women, which was why she always tried to be amusing when she was with one, but at home of course she didn't bother. Towards the end of the meal, however, her mother looked at her and said, 'Are you all right, dear; you look a little pale?' But before Nora could answer added disapprovingly, 'And you look as if you're putting on weight again. You can't be sticking to your diet.'

'I'm all right, Mummy, don't fuss,' her daughter

muttered, but Tressy noticed that she didn't eat any more of her lunch.

That afternoon they went out with Cris and Michel again, but now they weren't just four people any more, they were the usual two couples, or rather one couple and two odd people, because Cris made it very clear that he wanted to be with Tressy. They took a drive inland and stopped at a factory where they made crystallised fruits, Michel this time buying them each a basket, although he laughingly admitted he had a sweet tooth for them himself and ate quite a large portion.

Those two days were the start of several that each seemed better than the first. Tressy knew that she was falling for Cris and looked forward eagerly to seeing him, her heart doing somersaults at the most stupid things: when she first saw him, when they accidently touched, or just when she turned and found him watching her with that look of warm tenderness in his eyes. And all the time there was a feeling of heady excitement, as if things were happening to her she could do nothing about, even if she had wanted to. Mostly she didn't think about it, just let it happen, but all these emotions were very new to her and she was extremely unsure of herself, so was grateful that Cris seemed to understand and didn't make any demands on her, appearing content, too, to let things take their course. Once or twice, though, he showed signs of impatience when he tried to get Tressy alone for a while, but Nora, watching them like a hawk and wise now to that manoeuvre, dogged their footsteps and wouldn't leave them.

Evidence that his patience was wearing thin came one night when they came home after a visit to a night-club and Cris said a determined, 'Excuse us,' to the others and putting a hand under Tressy's elbow marched her round the house and into the garden.

'Hey, wait for me!' Hampered by her high heels, Tressy almost had to run to keep up with him.

'Sorry.' He slowed down a little, glancing over his shoulder to make sure they weren't being followed. 'Let's go down the path towards the beach.'

They went through the gate and Tressy expected him to take her to the spot they'd gone to on the night of the party, but they had only gone a little way down the path when he stopped in the deep shadow of a jacaranda tree and pulled her almost roughly into his arms. 'I've been waiting to do this for days,' he said thickly, and kissed her hungrily.

Tressy responded to his kiss without reserve, letting her emotions take over as she opened her mouth to his embrace. And it went to her head like vintage champagne as she became lost to everything but the surging need to be held closer in his arms, to feel his hard body against hers, to give as well as to take.

They kissed for long, timeless minutes and both were breathing raggedly when they at last drew apart. Cris put up an unsteady hand to her face. 'I think I got more than I bargained for then,' he said hoarsely.

Tressy smiled and moved her face against his hand. 'You took me by surprise.'

'Then I shall have to do so again—often.' With a small groan he drew her to him again. 'I want you to myself,' he told her huskily. 'If we have to go around with Nora and Michel for another day I shall go mad!'

Tressy laughed a little breathlessly. 'I'm beginning to believe you.'

'You'd better believe it,' he said forcefully. He bent to kiss her neck. 'Say you'll come out with me tomorrow.'

'What—what about Nora?' Tressy managed to say

between gasps as his mouth traced a line across her throat and up to her ear.

Reluctantly Cris raised his head and said, 'Nora's had enough time by now to realise that it's you I'm interested in. If she hasn't . . .' he shrugged, 'then I'm sorry. I've tried to let her down as gently as I know how.'

'You know, then—that she's in love with you?'

'I know she thinks she is,' Cris corrected. 'But it was entirely one-sided. I tried to avoid her once I realised the situation.'

Tressy frowned. 'But you kept coming round to the villa?'

'The first time because I didn't have much choice; I could envisage Nora and her parents looking for me and leaving messages all over the Riviera if I didn't. And after that . . .' He paused to pick up a lock of her hair and gently stroke it against his face. 'After that there began to be another attraction that drew me here.'

The look in his eyes left Tressy in no doubt that she was the attraction, and her heart jerked. 'Cris . . .'

'Yes.'

'I—I don't know . . .'

He put up a finger to close her lips, then replaced the finger with his mouth, kissing her lingeringly. 'Just say that you'll come out with me tomorrow. Just the two of us.'

'All right,' she agreed huskily, her voice somehow outside her control.

'Darling.'

He bent to kiss her again, but Tressy said, 'We'd better go back. Michel will be waiting. And I wouldn't put it past Nora to lock me out,' she added wryly.

'Despot! Don't you realise this is the first time I've

had you to myself in days?' But he turned and walked back towards the villa, holding her close against him so that she could feel the lean hardness of his body touching hers.

It wasn't until they were almost back at the house that a thought occurred to her and she stopped. 'Oh! We can't make it tomorrow,' she exclaimed. 'I've just remembered; we arranged to go to that festival in Nice.'

'Damn! I'd forgotten that. I suppose we'll have to go.' The disappointment was heavy in Cris's voice.

'But we could make it the day after, couldn't we?' For the first time she put her hands on his shoulders and reached up to kiss him of her own accord. She felt a shudder of emotion run through him, and then his hands were on her hips, holding her close.

'Tomorrow is going to be a hell of a long day,' he told her when he eventually let her go.

Michel was waiting by the car, smoking a cigarette and by no means impatient at being kept waiting so long. Cris kissed her goodbye in front of him and then made sure that Nora hadn't locked her out before they drove away.

Half afraid that her cousin might be waiting up to have a go at her, Tressy was relieved to see the place in darkness and crept up to her room, to fall asleep with the rosy promise of wonderful days ahead of her.

To everyone's surprise, Nora seemed to be her old self again the next day, chatting away and laughing at the smallest thing, but today all her attention was concentrated on Michel. She quite openly flirted with him, holding on to his arm and draping herself against him whenever she could. Michel took it well and seemed to be enjoying himself, and Tressy was so relieved that Nora wasn't sulking any more that she failed to notice the brittleness behind the other girl's laughter or the desperateness in her actions as she tried to make Cris jealous. She did notice, though, when Nora took off her dress to sunbathe on the boat that she was looking thin again, her bones starting to show, which was rather strange, because she'd always seemed to eat quite well when they were all out together.

Tressy half hoped that, now Nora was concentrating on Michel, there would be a chance for her and Cris to be alone for a while, but Nora still tagged along wherever they went. To compensate, though, Cris was more open in his attentions to Tressy, seldom letting her leave his side and behaving with a possessiveness that a couple of weeks ago she would have objected to strongly but now rather enjoyed. His eyes, too, carried messages that sent an excited tingle down her spine. Tomorrow; tomorrow they would be alone. Although how Cris expected to get away from Nora she couldn't imagine.

But she needn't have worried; Cris managed it very adroitly when he took them back to the villa that night, by saying authoritatively, 'I think it's about time we split up. I'm taking Tressy out with me tomorrow.'

As if on cue, which it probably was, Michel turned to Nora and said, '*Bon*. Perhaps you would come for a trip on my yacht, *ma chère*?'

But Nora had stiffened and was looking at Cris. 'I thought we were supposed to be a foursome?'

'Foursomes don't last indefinitely,' Cris answered gently, and put his arm round Tressy as if to emphasise his point.

'She's supposed to be *my* companion,' Nora pointed out waspishly. 'That's what she's *paid* for.'

Cris's jaw tightened, but he said patiently, 'In that case she's about due for a day off. And you know that you'll be quite okay with Michel.'

'I don't . . .' Nora pulled herself up before she was openly rude. 'I don't know if I can make it tomorrow,' she amended, her voice unsteady.

'But it will make me very happy if you will let me be your escort tomorrow, *ma chérie*,' Michel told her, picking up her hand and kissing it.

'Thank you. But—but I'm not sure. G-goodnight.'

The two men said good night to her, then Cris turned to Tressy. 'Good night, darling.' And he kissed her lingeringly on the mouth, his eyes laughing at the look on her face when he let her go. Tressy turned rather dazedly to see Nora's reaction, but the other girl had already gone inside.

Tressy waved the men off before going inside herself, eager for tomorrow to come and yet in some ways enjoying the anticipation and wanting to prolong it. She tried to tell herself not to expect too much from this friendship with Cris, after all she'd only known him for about a month and she'd quite definitely disliked him at first, but she had seen him nearly every day, and now . . . How did she really feel about him? Tressy only knew that she had never felt like this before, and whether it was love or not, it felt pretty good. She knew that she liked being with him and to have him near, and when he kissed her she didn't want him to stop. He would, she thought, make a fantastic lover and, in the long run, an even better friend. She smiled to herself; somehow she didn't think it was friendship he was interested in.

The same sense of excited anticipation was still there when Tressy woke the next morning, and she hurried to get ready. Cris had said that she could crew for him and they would take the boat westward down the coast to a group of islands, the Isles of Gold, he'd called them, a few miles out to sea. He hadn't had to tell her that there they would try to find a beach you could only reach by sea, a beach they would have all to themselves.

The others were already at breakfast and Aunt Grace was now telling Nora to eat because she looked so peaky. Nora resisted, but her mother made her eat two of the rolls. Tressy fully expected to be taken to task this morning, but when nothing was said, realised that Nora couldn't have told her parents that she and Cris were going out together. Wounded pride, perhaps? As soon as she had finished eating, Nora excused herself and went indoors. Uncle Jack and Aunt Grace were all ready to go on a trip into Italy with the Youngs and they left at the same time, leaving Tressy to clear the breakfast things as it was the maid's day off and then run upstairs, eager to get ready for Cris, although she was much too early; he wasn't coming to pick her up until ten.

The door to Nora's bedroom was ajar and as she passed it Tressy heard some strange choking noises. She hesitated, then knocked, but there was no answer and the strange noises came again. Tressy pushed open the door and looked inside. 'Nora?' The bedroom was empty, but the adjoining bathroom door stood open and the sounds came from there. 'Nora, are you all right?' Tressy looked into the bathroom and saw her cousin leaning over the loo with her fingers down her throat, making herself sick. 'What on earth? Are you ill?'

Tressy went towards her, ready to help, but Nora straightened up, her face flaming. 'Go away! Get out of here!' she yelled.

'But if you're . . .' Then Tressy stopped as realisation dawned. 'You're doing it on purpose! But why?'

'Why?' Nora laughed, her voice high and unnatural. 'He prefers thin girls, that's *why*.'

'Oh, God! You're doing this for Cris.' Tressy stared at her, appalled.

'Yes, of course I'm doing it for him. I'd do anything for him. Don't you understand? I'm in love with him.'

'But—but Nora, he doesn't—he's not . . .'

'No, because you've stolen him from me!' Nora suddenly sprang across the room and took hold of Tressy's shoulders, shaking her violently. Her eyes were wild and there were traces of vomit round her mouth. 'You bitch! You stole him from me! But he'll see through you. He'll see what a tart you are and he'll come back to me. You'll see—you'll see!'

'Nora, don't. You'll make yourself ill.' Tressy tried to push her away, but Nora was a big girl and she seemed to have a mad strength, shaking Tressy till her teeth rattled.

'We would have been engaged by now if you hadn't thrown yourself at him. Pretending to dislike him so that he'd take an interest in you. You filthy bitch!'

'Stop it! That isn't true.'

'Oh, yes, it damn well is.' Nora suddenly gave her a violent push and Tressy went flying backwards out of the bathroom, ending up on the bedroom floor and glad that it was thickly carpeted. Quickly she got to her feet when she saw that Nora was coming after her. 'But you needn't think he'll marry you, because he won't!' she shouted. 'Men like him don't marry bastards!'

Tressy stared at her, suddenly feeling sick herself. 'What—what do you mean?'

'Oh, don't look so damn innocent. You know darn well that your mother tricked your father into marrying her—if he was your father,' Nora sneered insultingly. 'No wonder he walked out on her—it must have been hell trying to live with a whore. And you needn't think you can trap Cris the same way, because I'll tell him. And when he sees that you're just like your mother, he'll never want to see you again!'

Tressy's legs felt too weak to hold her and she groped for the edge of the bed and slumped down on it. She didn't doubt what Nora had said even for a moment; she could never have made up something like that, not in the temper she was in. To know that she was the cause of her mother's unhappy marriage was a great shock; she felt as if someone had punched her in the ribs and driven all the breath out of her, and she could only sit and stare dumbly at her cousin's maddened face. But unsavoury as it was, this was ancient history and she was certain that Cris would look upon it as such. And most of the insults Nora had hurled at her were untrue anyway; she didn't even know if she wanted to marry Cris, let alone trap him into it. So she stood up again and said forcefully, 'For heaven's sake calm down, Nora. You're making yourself ill. Look, I'm sorry if you're upset, but I didn't set out to catch Cris, you know that. It just happened. Not that anything really has happened, not yet.'

'And it won't,' Nora said viciously. 'Because you're not going to go out with him again.'

'Like hell,' Tressy retorted. 'I shall do as I like. Your father may pay me, Nora, but that doesn't give you the right to run my life.'

Which was entirely the wrong thing to say. Nora glared at her, her face suffused with rage. She looked wildly round the room, then ran over to the dressing table, grabbing up a pair of scissors and opening the blades, holding them like a double-ended knife. Then she swung triumphantly round to Tressy. 'You filthy bitch! You shan't have him, you shan't!'

Her face ashen, Tressy backed away, holding out her hands to ward Nora off, although there was such a crazed look on the other girl's face that it would have been futile.

Nora laughed, her voice high and unnatural. 'Oh, yes, you're afraid of me now, aren't you, you bitch, with your red hair and your big eyes. But I'm not going to hurt you, because I know that that wouldn't bring Cris back to me. *You're* going to give him up. Because if you don't . . .' She raised her right hand holding the scissors high in the air and her voice rose to a shriek, 'I'll kill myself, and it'll be your fault. Because he's mine! He's mine. He's mine!' And on the word mine, she brought the scissors flashing down three times, slashing across her left wrist, the bright blood spurting out as she screamed the words. Then she stopped suddenly, dropping the scissors and staring at her wrist, the lack of sound somehow louder than her screams. Her face deathly white, she turned to Tressy and said, almost calmly. '*You see?* You see I mean it?'

CHAPTER SEVEN

'OH God!' Somehow Tressy forced her legs to move and she ran into the bathroom and snatched up a clean towel, then wrapped it tightly round Nora's wrist.

Her cousin stood passively, as if all the wildness had drained out of her, but when Tressy led her to a chair and made her sit down, she shot out her good hand and caught hold of Tressy's arm. 'There are lots of ways to commit suicide, and I'll do it, I swear it, if you don't promise to give him up. I can't live without him. And you don't even love him. Do you? Do you?' she insisted.

Tressy was on her knees in front of her, holding the bloodstained towel tightly against Nora's wrist. Looking up at the other girl with horrified eyes, she had to say honestly, 'I—I don't know.'

'So you'll give him up?' Nora said feverishly. 'Promise me you'll give him up!'

There was blood on her own hands. Tressy looked down at it and then at the splashes round the room where Nora had swung her arm. 'Yes, all right,' she agreed tiredly.

'Say it!' Nora commanded, her fingers biting painfully into Tressy's arm.

'I promise I'll give him up. I'll go back to England tomorrow. Nora, you must let me send for an ambulance.'

But her cousin ignored her. 'No, you mustn't go back home; he might go after you. You've got to stay here and convince him that you're not interested in him any more.'

'Yes, all right, whatever you say.' Tressy was beginning to be afraid that she'd bleed to death. 'We *must* get an ambulance.'

'No, just send for that doctor Mummy had recommended to her.' Now that she had got her own way, Nora seemed to be fully in command of herself again, still deathly pale, but with a triumphant look in her dark-rimmed eyes.

The doctor came very quickly when he heard the fear in Tressy's voice, but fortunately the cuts weren't very deep and didn't even need stitches. Nora lied and told him she'd cut herself with the electric carving knife, which he didn't believe but was willing to accept for the fat fee that Nora paid him.

He had only been gone a few minutes when the doorbell rang again. It was a few minutes to ten.

'That will be Cris,' murmured Tressy. The two girls looked at each other. 'I'll—I'll go and tell him.'

'*No*. I'll see him. I don't trust you.' Nora looked at herself anxiously in the mirror and quickly added some blusher to give colour to her pale cheeks. Tressy had helped her to change out of her bloodstained dress and there was no sign, other than the dressing on her wrist, that anything had happened. She went over to the door and looked back. 'You can clean up this room; do what you're paid to do for a change,' she said insultingly.

Obediently Tressy bent to pick up the dress and towel, but then dropped them again and went over to the window, open wide to let in any breeze there might be. Nora's room was at the front of the house, almost over the main door, and she heard her cousin quite clearly as she greeted Cris.

Her voice bright, Nora said, 'Hallo, Crispin, how are you? Isn't it a lovely day again?'

'It is indeed. Is Tressy ready?' Cris's deep tones

answered, the eagerness in his voice scarcely concealed.

'Oh, dear!' Nora gave an embarrassed laugh and Tressy's fists clenched as she could imagine the act her cousin was putting on. 'I'm afraid she won't be going with you today.'

'Why? Is she ill?' Cris asked sharply.

'Oh no, nothing like that. Actually, I'm the one who's in the wars. I scalded myself when I was helping to make breakfast this morning.'

'I'm sorry. I hope it isn't too serious?'

'No, but of course I won't be able to swim until it's better, which is rather a bore.'

'Yes. You were telling me about Tressy,' he prompted.

'Well, I was rather hoping not to.' Nora pretended to be sympathetic. 'I'm afraid she's gone out with someone else.'

'Someone else?' Cris's voice was incredulous. 'Who?'

'Some man she knew back in London. He phoned her yesterday and she contacted him after we got back last night. It seems he's over here on holiday and she went off to meet him this morning.'

'Didn't she leave any message for me?'

'I'm afraid not. Er—I'm sorry to say this of my own cousin, Crispin, but Tressy really isn't terribly reliable, you know. She quite often lets people down.'

'Really? She hadn't struck me that way. Are you quite sure of this?'

'Certainly I am.' Nora sounded offended. 'As a matter of fact, Tressy takes after her mother; she wasn't very good with men either.'

Up in the bedroom, Tressy clenched her fists; if Nora made one more remark about her mother she'd go down there, promise or no promise!

But Nora was saying. 'I do apologise if you've been inconvenienced, Crispin. I suppose your boat is all ready to go?' She left the unspoken suggestion hanging in the air.

Cris, though, ignored it. 'Did she say when she would be back?' he demanded abruptly.

'Oh, no. She'll come back when she feels like it, I suppose—if she comes back at all tonight. She seemed very keen to see this man.'

'I see,' Cris answered grimly.

There was silence for a few moments and then Nora said cajolingly, 'Crispin, I'm at a loose end myself today. Couldn't I come on your trip with you?'

'I know that Michel is going to phone you later to see if you'd care to go out with him.'

'But I don't want to go out with Michel. I—I'd much rather go with you. Please!' she added in a tone that gave away her feelings completely.

'Sorry, Nora.' Crispin didn't hesitate with his refusal. 'If Tressy can't make it today, then I have several business matters I can attend to. Tell Tressy I'll call her tomorrow, will you?'

'You still want to see her—after she's stood you up?' Nora asked in hurt and outrage.

'I'm quite sure she had a good reason for doing so— and I'd like to hear it from her. Make sure she gets my message, won't you?' There was a distinct warning in his tone. 'Goodbye, Nora.'

'It's Leonora. My name's Leonora.'

But Cris's footsteps could be heard stepping briskly to his car.

Slowly Tressy moved away from the window and sat down in a chair. It had been very hard to stand there in silence when she'd longed to lean out of the window and call, 'Here I am!' Only the memory of those brilliant splashes of blood from Nora's wrist had held her back. Because when it came to it, she found that she did care about not seeing Cris again—very much. She felt wretched and bitter and in that moment hated her cousin, unable to find any sympathy now for her unrequited feelings.

She was still sitting in the chair when Nora came back, her pace far slower now than it had been when she had run down to open the door. Nora looked round the room and started to say, 'Why haven't you . . .' but then saw the look on Tressy's face and her voice died away.

'Congratulations,' Tressy said scathingly into the silence. 'I hadn't realised what a consummate liar you are. Where did you learn, I wonder? At your precious convent school you're always bragging about? Tell me, how did you think of what to tell him so quickly—or did you have it all worked out beforehand?'

Nora flushed. 'That isn't true! It was the obvious excuse to give.' She gathered herself up. 'And you're supposed to be cleaning this room up; you don't want my parents to see it, do you? I'll tell them it's your fault.'

'I'm quite sure you will.' Tressy stood up. 'I'm quite sure you're capable of lying your head off to get what you want. But I couldn't care less. And you can clean the room yourself.'

'But I can't; my wrist is hurting.'

'It wasn't hurting when you offered yourself on a plate to Cris, was it?' Tressy returned coolly, walking over to the door. 'Only it didn't do you any good, did it? He turned you down flat.'

Nora's face contorted and she looked as if she was going to either burst into tears or go wild again. 'Don't you dare speak to me like that! You know what will happen if you upset me; I'll kill myself.'

'I should be very careful, if I were you, Nora,'

Tressy told her, her voice icy. 'The way you're behaving I'm beginning not to care very much whether you live or die.' And she walked out of the room.

The villa suddenly seemed like a prison and she couldn't stand it any longer. The scooter was still in its hiding place, repaired and returned a couple of weeks ago, but she hadn't used it since. Now, she collected her things and drove it out on to the main road, much busier with traffic now that it was July and the French nation had started its mass exodus to the sea, most of them, Tressy thought, either using this road or parked on both sides of it. As soon as she could, she turned off the main road and just followed her nose, not much caring where she went, just wanting to get as far away from Nora as possible. After about an hour's ride, she came to a field entrance and parked the scooter behind a hedge, then walked to the edge of a small wood and sat in the shade of a tree, looking down a sloping meadow to a landscape of lush green fields with a small village in the valley and an old bridge over a river, and beyond high hills that rose steeply towards the cloudless blue sky.

She felt thoroughly fed up and miserable, thinking of what it would have been like to be with Cris today. She thought about him, wondering what he was doing and whether he would really phone tomorrow after the lies Nora had told him. But yes, if he'd said he'd phone then he would keep his word. Probably only to be met by another load of Nora's lies as she tried to discredit Tressy for ever in his eyes. Savagely she pulled at some pieces of grass. Wishing, wishing. But wishing never did anyone any good; she could hear her mother saying it now. Her mother, who had always taught her that her father had been in the wrong. Only maybe it hadn't been like that at all. Lying back,

Tressy gazed up at the sky, remembering the way that Cris had looked at her and touched her that day they had gone to Menton and had those few precious hours alone together. All, it seemed now, that they were destined to have. Because for all she'd told Nora to get on with it, her cousin's irrational behaviour this morning had frightened Tressy to death. Shudders ran through her as she remembered, and she knew that there was no way she could ever take the risk of Nora doing it again, but in reality this time. She must be crazy about Cris if she could inflict such violence on herself in a desperate attempt to try and get him back. If she loved him that much, and if love drove her to that despair, then all Tressy could do was keep out of the way and let Nora try to catch him. God, it must be terrible to be in love, to feel as intensely as that! Tressy blinked at the sky and thought that her own feelings were pretty intense at the moment. But she was tough, she'd get over it, whereas Nora, who had always had everything she ever wanted . . . Deliberately she pushed aside thoughts of what Nora would do if she didn't make any headway with Cris. And Tressy didn't think she would. Not now. No matter how much Nora blackened her name. All that would happen would be that they'd both lose him. If he was ever to be won. And that wasn't certain. Nothing was certain any more. Only the sky, the sun and trees. Stupid tears pricked her eyes and she angrily blinked them back, glad that she was tough, so very tough.

Nora hadn't gone out with Michel; when Tressy got back to the villa late that afternoon she was lying on the settee with Aunt Grace fussing over her because of her 'poor scalded arm', and Tressy immediately got a good telling off for leaving her and for not doing the washing up. It seemed Nora had piously told her mother she'd scalded herself boiling up a kettle to do the washing up herself. Tressy just looked at them and went into the kitchen to make herself a sandwich.

The next morning Nora hovered by the phone, making sure she picked it up when Cris called. She must have told him more lies, but this time Tressy didn't stay around to hear, instead taking the scooter into Monte Carlo. Taking care to keep away from the harbour area or any places where Cris might happen to be, Tressy wandered around the streets, window-shopping. Thanks to Cris taking her out so much, she had spent very little of the wages Uncle Jack paid her and she felt like buying something to cheer herself up, but the clothes here were all so expensive compared to the shops in England that her native sense of thrift held her back. But there was one leather goods shop that had a sale on and in the window was a beautiful snakeskin handbag with a long gold-coloured chain. It cost six hundred francs, which worked out at over fifty pounds in English money. Tressy gazed at it enviously for quite a time and then walked on. She had never spent that much on a handbag and there were lots of more practical uses that she needed money for. But it was a gorgeous bag!

It was very hot that day, still and close. Tressy spent the rest of it on the beach in Nice, sweltering in the heat. As she gazed up at the sky an aeroplane flew slowly down the length of the beach, towing a sign behind it asking holidaymakers to adopt an abandoned dog or cat. Tressy laughed mirthlessly; how about adopting an unwanted girl? She could use some tender, loving care right now. That made her think of her mother, and she wondered whether she had deliberately tricked her father into marrying her. And had it made her bitter when everything backfired on her and she was left with a child on her hands to bring up alone? Certainly her mother had never been a demonstrative woman; she had worked hard and done her best for Tressy, but more out of duty than love. So Tressy, in her turn, had no idea how to show love or even how to recognise it.

A French boy came over and started chatting her up. He was harmless, and she let him buy her a pizza. He was staying at a camp site near Vence and wanted her to go back there with him, but she told him she was working and had to get back, so he gave her his telephone number and they parted amicably enough. But it was strange, although he was nice, Tressy felt completely detached from him and couldn't have cared less whether he talked to her or not. He was of medium height and fair, but she had grown used to a tall dark man walking beside her, his arm casually across her shoulders, and now she felt incomplete when she walked alone. Tressy realised, with surprise, that she felt lonely, an emotion she had never experienced before because she was used to being on her own. She hadn't been close enough to anyone to miss them before; never once had she missed her mother on the few occasions she had been away from home for any length of time. But she was missing Cris now, and it was as unwelcome as it was unfamiliar.

Maybe it was just as well that Nora had brought things to an end between them, she told herself. It wouldn't have done to get too deeply involved with Cris. Holiday romances never lasted, everyone knew that. Emotions that burst into flame in the heat of the sun soon died in the chill of winter. And she and Cris had nothing in common—except a heady physical attraction that made her want to touch and be touched. And what was physical attraction but a passing thing? It didn't last. Nothing lasted. Nothing was for ever.

Michel was at the villa when she got back. Tressy

recognised his Renault and was careful to go into the house by the kitchen door. She wasn't particularly hungry but fixed herself a fresh orange juice to take up to her room, then left a note to say that she was in, knowing Aunt Grace would find it when she came to make her milk drink as she always did before going to bed. There was the sound of voices coming from the drawing-room, but Tressy wasn't quite sure whether it was the television or not. As she made her way up the stairs, the door to the drawing-room opened and Michel came out into the large hall, followed by Nora. Tressy quickened her footsteps, hoping to reach the flight to the next floor before he saw her. But he looked up and called her name.

Glancing down, she said, 'Oh, hi, Michel,' and went quickly on her way.

'Wait!' Michel came bounding up the stairs after her. 'I must speak to you.'

'Some other time, huh? I'm tired right now.' She tried to move on, but he caught her arm.

'Cris is worried about you,' he said as Nora came up behind him to listen, her eyes giving warning messages.

'Is he?' Tressy answered inadequately, unable to think what to say.

'Will you meet him somewhere?'

'I'm afraid I'm pretty busy right now, Michel.' Freeing her arm, she edged away.

'But will you not telephone him, then?'

'Oh, sure. When I have the time. Good night.' And she escaped up the flight of stairs to the top floor and locked herself in her room, leaving Nora to grab Michel and stop him following her again.

It was terribly hot, the air close and sultry. The efficient air-conditioning in the villa didn't extend to the maid's room, so Tressy pushed the window open as wide as it would go and tried to settle down to sleep, pushing aside the coverlet and having only a thin sheet over her. But even this was too much. Sitting up, she pulled off her thin nightdress and lay naked, her body wet with perspiration, longing for some air. But it wasn't only the heat, her mind was too active, too full of thoughts for her to relax and let sleep come. After about an hour of tossing and turning, Tressy got up and put on a towelling robe and sandals, then crept downstairs, careful not to wake her aunt and uncle who had come in shortly after Michel had left.

The air-conditioned rooms felt almost cold after the stifling heat of her room, and Tressy contemplated spending the rest of the night on a settee; it would certainly be more comfortable. Wandering over to the French windows, she looked out and saw that the night had completely clouded over, the sky black and menacing. It seemed strange not to see the moon and stars. Tressy unlatched the windows and went outside, stepping into the electric blanket of heat, immediately feeling sweaty and sticky again. There was no moon reflected in the still waters of the swimming pool, but it still looked infinitely inviting. Without hesitation, Tressy stepped out of her robe and waded down the circular steps into the pool. It was so cool, heavenly. Lowering herself into the water, she swam slowly down the length of the pool, then turned on her back and floated, gazing up at the dark, heavy sky. From not far away came a reverberation of thunder and she gave a sigh of relief; perhaps a storm would lift this oppressive heat. She swam for about twenty minutes or so and then came out, the water running down her silky skin as she climbed the steps. Lifting up her arms, she stood poised on the edge as she tilted her head back and squeezed water out of her hair, her tall, slim body outlined by a sudden flash of lightning.

'Hallo, Tressy.'

The soft words came from the other side of the pool and she swung round, although she knew the voice at once. Cris moved forward a little so that she could see him more clearly. How long he'd been there she had no idea. There was no point in being embarrassed; he had seen everything there was to see, but Tressy stooped down gracefully and picked up her robe, putting it on before she answered him.

'Do you make a habit of this kind of thing?' she asked tartly. Then, when he didn't reply, 'What do you want?'

'To see you.' His voice had hardened. 'To find out for myself just what's going on.'

There was a great rumble of thunder and the lightning flashed again, the whole sky a battlefield. It lit Cris's grim features, and Tressy suddenly wanted to run to him and take that look from his face, to hold him close and feel his arms about her, to make everything all right again. But she couldn't do that, she didn't dare take the risk. She was going to have to be hard, hard on him and on herself, and she was sharply aware that it was going to hurt appallingly. But this moment had been inevitable from the instant Nora had brought those scissors slashing down. Stepping into her sandals, Tressy said as coldly and steadily as she could manage, 'You saw Nora, didn't you?'

'I saw her, yes. She told me that you were going out with another man. I didn't believe her,' he added harshly.

Tressy's heart began to thump painfully as she wished she could end this and go inside, but Cris was standing between her and the house. 'Why should she lie?' she prevaricated, edging towards the building.

'I think we both know why Nora would lie.' He

waited for her to deny it, then said bleakly, 'I take it, then, that it's true?'

'So what if it is?' Tressy's chin came up. 'I go out with who I like.'

'And stand up those you don't like, obviously,' Cris said with bitter self-mockery. 'But tell me, just for the record, why the hell did you say you'd go out with me in the first place if you dislike me so much?'

She shrugged, acting now for all she was worth so that this would soon be over. 'Because you were a free meal ticket, of course. I never turn down a free meal.'

'From anyone?'

'Not from anyone like you,' she retorted, deliberately making her tone insulting. She had been trying to get towards the house, but at this Cris came round the head of the pool and strode towards her, making her instinctively back away.

'So it was all a game to you, was it?' He caught her arm, his face contorted with anger. 'It didn't mean a thing. I was just a means of free entertainment until your boy-friend turned up. Or should I say your lover? Is he your lover?' He shook her arm, gripping hard.

'Mind your own damn business!'

His grip tightened, his fingers digging into her flesh. 'What's so wonderful about him? Is he so bloody marvellous in bed? Is that it?' He caught her other wrist, his voice rising in fury as the storm began to break around them. 'My God, I was all wrong about you, wasn't I? I thought you were soft and vulnerable underneath that veneer of hardness. But you're tough all right, really hard! And I handled you all wrong. Tough girls like being mastered, so they say, but I treated you like Dresden china, afraid you'd break and be scared off. But maybe this is what you really wanted all along.' And he pulled her roughly into his arms, bending her back so that she was braced against his taut body, his hand in her wet hair as he brought his mouth down on hers, taking her lips in a mixture of fury and revenge, caring for nothing but the need to dominate and possess.

Tressy tried to cry out, but her mouth was locked under his and she made only futile sounds of fierce resentment. She beat at his chest with clenched fists, but he was as impervious as a punch bag, intent only on taking his anger out on her. Somehow she managed to kick his ankle and he swore at her, his kiss hardening and hurting her as he forced her mouth open. Tressy tried to turn her head away, hating him for what he was doing to her, but he held her captive, taking a feverish enjoyment out of her helplessness. But maybe she wasn't entirely helpless—from somewhere she dragged up the memory of a TV programme she'd seen on self-defence, and brought the side of her hand up against his throat. Cris's head went back and he automatically stepped away from her, his grip loosening.

'You animal! You rotten, stinking pig!' She lashed out at him, catching him on the side of his face. She did it in reaction to her own anger, but it was entirely the wrong thing to say and do. If she had reasoned with him, Cris would have calmed down at once, but her words pushed him over the edge of the precarious hold on his temper and she cried out with fear and turned to run as she saw the look of pure rage on his face as he lunged towards her.

Impossible to get to the house—Tressy ran to the only other means of escape, out of the gate and down the path leading towards the beach, the thunder and lightning breaking immediately overhead now and the first heavy, scalding drops of rain hitting the parched ground. At the first bend she glanced back and saw

Cris coming after her. With a sob she plunged on down the steeply zig-zagging path, ignoring the risk of a twisted ankle, the skirts of her robe flying open. She jumped the last few feet to the beach, and then looked round wildly like a cornered animal, not knowing which way to go for the best. Turning to the left, Tressy began to run along the empty beach, the usually placid sea a surging maelstrom of pounding waves, the rain blinding her.

Her foot caught on a stone and she stumbled, but somehow managed to save herself and run on, but the next moment Cris caught her and jerked her violently round to face him, his breath ragged and gasping. Then she was fighting him in all earnestness, knowing her danger, using nails, teeth, feet, hurting him as much as she could. Deliberately he tripped her and they fell to the ground, fighting savagely as they rolled on the wet sand. As they struggled Tressy's robe came open and a great, jagged flash of forked lightning revealed her to him as Cris lay half on top of her.

'You bitch! Oh God, you beautiful bitch!'

Time and sound seemed to be suspended as he reached out and touched her breast, his hand infinitely gentle. Tressy shuddered on a wave of sexuality and stared into Cris's face. Then she gave a low moan of desire, and pulled him down towards her as a great roar of thunder broke above their heads.

Now rage turned to a primitive passion and their fighting was of a different kind as they lay on the rain-soaked beach. For a few minutes Tressy felt the raindrops drumming against her bare back as she tore at his shirt, but then Cris swung her under him and she cried out as he explored her with hand and mouth, her hands twisted in his hair or digging into his shoulders. He released her for a brief moment and when he turned to her again she felt the smooth nakedness of his skin against her own. Her body arched towards him, eager to feel the thrust of his male hardness, her whole being on fire with the hunger for love.

'Tressy. Oh, Tressy!' His voice was hoarse and rasping, drawn out into a groan.

'I want you. I want you to make love to me.' Her frenzied plea reached him through the raging storm and he put his hands on either side of her head, staring down into her face before he lunged forward and took her in a ravaging invasion of savage hunger, his voice joining hers in a rising cry of sensuality as his body surged in a great climax of passion.

They lay there unmoving, arms and legs in a tangle of limbs as the rain beat down on them, then Cris lifted his head and kissed her, a long kiss of tender gratitude. Tressy returned it, with a passion she had not realised she possessed. But it had an unexpected effect, because she felt Cris harden and his body begin to move against her. She gasped, and he gave a soft, triumphant laugh. 'What did you expect?'

He made love to her more slowly this time, his first overpowering need diminished so that he could give as well as take. And he gave in abundance, making love to her with an expertise that lifted her close to the heights and away again several times before he at last gave her frantic body the satisfaction she begged him for.

Exhausted now, Tressy lay in his arms as the storm moved on, the thunder becoming distant and only the sound of the waves and their own uneven breathing breaking the silence. And with the passing of the storm came sanity and the realisation of what she had done—and of what Nora would do if she ever found out. Horrified, Tressy pulled herself free of Cris's arms and stood up unsteadily. She was covered in wet sand, it was in her hair and sticking to her skin. Walking down to the sea, she waded in and dived as soon as the water was deep enough, turning on her back to wash the sand out of her hair. There was a splash as Cris dived through a wave and swam to join her, but Tressy deliberately went under the surface to avoid him and swam back towards the shore. Then she ran to put on her sandals and her uncomfortably wet and sandy robe.

'Hey, wait for me!' Cris was wading towards her through the shallows farther down the beach.

'No! You stay away from me!' Her yell halted him in his tracks and he stood and gazed at her disbelievingly. 'You've got what you wanted. Now leave me alone!' And then, hating herself for having submitted to him so weakly and terribly afraid of the effect it might have on her cousin, she took her fear and confusion out on Cris, shouting in genuine fury, 'I hate you! I hate you!' Then she turned and ran back up the path, leaving him still staring after her.

CHAPTER EIGHT

TRESSY reached the house safely, praying that the storm hadn't woken anyone. The last thing she wanted was for someone to look out of a window and see her, but her relations were all heavy sleepers and she reached her room safely. With a sigh of relief she took off the sodden robe and dropped it into the handbasin, then towelled herself dry and got into bed, almost feeling chilly now after the earlier heat. She was half afraid that Cris might do something crazy, like ring the front door bell until someone answered it and then demand to see her, but after a very tense half hour in which nothing happened, she was able to relax a little and try to think what to do.

The most important thing, of course, was to make sure that Nora never found out. She tried to concentrate on how best to do this, but her thoughts kept going back to their tempestuous lovemaking on the beach. Why had she stopped fighting and given in to him? Why? It had been a mad and crazy thing to do. She should have gone on resisting him. But wouldn't that have annoyed him so much that he would have taken her by force? And what was the point in fighting him when she had wanted it so badly? Tressy gave an inward moan as she remembered how much she had wanted him and how wonderful it had been. She still ached from his sexual domination, but she didn't feel used; her body was alive now as it had never been. In the moment when Tressy had told him she hated him, she had meant it, but now she realised that her feelings were far opposite to hate, and she was filled with a great sadness. What a mess. Oh God, what an unholy mess!

Cris phoned the villa the next morning after breakfast. Tressy was sitting on the terrace giving Aunt Grace a manicure, but couldn't have reached the phone even if she'd wanted to, because Nora made sure she grabbed it first. The phone call was no surprise, but Nora's reaction was. She came out on to the terrace beaming her head off. 'That was Crispin,' she informed them with relish. 'He's asked me to have lunch with him. You'll have to do my hair and nails, Tressy, and then you can make sure the things I want to wear are properly pressed.'

She went gleefully up to her room, to decide which clothes she wanted, leaving Tressy with her thoughts in chaos. Was this Cris's way of getting back at her? But she just couldn't believe it of him. He wasn't the vindictive type. But after last night . . . Who could tell what reaction her walking out on him could have provoked? It seemed that Nora was meeting him in Monte Carlo, and she left by taxi, her face flushed and eyes sparkling, convinced that her desperate gamble had paid off and that Cris was hers for the taking now.

Tressy, however, had dark circles under her eyes and felt deathly tired, not having slept at all last night. When she at last had the place to herself, she pulled a lounger with a thick mattress over beside the pool and took off the slacks and shirt she had been wearing all day, looking ruefully at the bruises on her skin that they had been hiding. Sleep claimed her almost instantly, so she didn't hear Nora come back a couple of hours or so later, not waking until almost five o'clock when the sun had gone round and she lay in the shadow of a pine tree.

After making herself something to eat, Tressy

wandered into the house and went upstairs to shower, thinking rather bleakly that Nora's lunch date with Cris was turning into an all-day affair. Perhaps he had taken her back to his boat and they had gone to some deserted cove. Would he make love to Nora, too? Or would he prefer to make her his wife than his mistress? The idea was unbearable, and she ran upstairs, almost missing the fact that Nora's bedroom door was wide open. But something white lying on the floor caught her eye and she went in. It was the short-sleeved silk shirt and matching skirt that Nora had worn for her date. So she had been back, to change, presumably. If so, Cris must have brought her, and Tressy flushed as she wondered if he had looked at her while she lay asleep.

Automatically she bent to pick up the clothes—and then stared; both garments had been torn violently, leaving long jagged holes in the soft material. For a moment Tressy was too stunned to think, but then she saw Nora's scissors lying on the floor and realised that her cousin must have taken the clothes off and slashed them in a fit of temper. But why? What could have happened? And where was Nora now? Tressy sat down on the bed, trying to figure it out and dreadfully afraid that Nora might be upset enough to do something desperate again. But the fact that she had only slashed her clothes to pieces and not herself seemed to be a hopeful sign. Tressy sighed; short of phoning Cris and asking him what had happened, there was no way she was going to find out until Nora turned up again. And she certainly didn't intend to phone Cris. She looked down at the ruined garments; it was an outfit that Nora had bought in Nice and had cost nearly three hundred pounds. It was one of the few things Nora had that Tressy really liked and she could have cried at the waste, but she took it downstairs and hid it in the rubbish bin so that Aunt Grace wouldn't see it. Then all she could do was sit and gnaw her fingers, hoping against hope that Nora would be all right, while she waited for her to come home.

By eleven that evening Tressy was getting really worried, and at midnight her aunt and uncle came home, reasonably early for once and looking as if they had had a row. They asked her where Nora was and Tressy replied, truthfully, that she hadn't seen her since she'd gone to meet Cris, and they went to bed satisfied that their daughter was in the hands of an eligible man. Tressy had been strongly tempted to tell them of her fears, but that meant coming clean about Nora's slashed wrist, and she was reluctant to get Nora into trouble when there might be some innocent explanation for her lateness. But as soon as they went upstairs, she telephoned Michel at his apartment. Luckily he was in.

'Oh, hi. This is Tressy. Sorry to bother you, but does Nora happen to be with you? Oh, you haven't Er—have you seen Cris at all today? He's with you now? No! No, I don't want to speak to him,' she said hastily. 'But could you ask him if he knows where Nora is?'

But Michel relayed the news that Cris had put Nora into a taxi to take her home at about two-thirty and hadn't seen her since. 'Is there anything the matter?' Michel asked. 'I would like to help if I can.'

'Thanks, but it's nothing, really. I expect she's met some friends or something. Good night.' She put the receiver down quickly, afraid he might insist.

The clock clicked slowly round for another interminable hour and struck one on a dismal note. It was still early of course by Monte Carlo standards, but in the circumstances ... Picking up the phone again she had Nora paged in all the night-clubs and restaurants they had visited with Cris and Michel, but drew a complete blank. So then there was nothing else for it, and running up to her room, Tressy put on a pair of jeans and a lightweight sweater, then left a note in case Nora turned up, before letting herself out of the house and hurrying to get the scooter.

Looking for one young girl in night-time Monte Carlo was like looking for a very small needle in a very large haystack, but Tressy was nothing if not resourceful and scoured the streets systematically, getting off the bike to go and look in cafés and discos. After an hour she went back to the house, but there was still no sign of her cousin.

By this time Tressy was getting pretty desperate, but she decided to have one more try. The pavements were slightly less crowded now except where knots of people were coming out of different night-spots. Tressy looked at them as closely as she could as she rode by, but some people glared at her suspiciously, thinking that she was one of the young thieves who rode up on scooters and motor bikes to snatch the handbags of women walking near the pavement edge. Once she thought she had found Nora, but it turned out to be a Scandinavian girl of about the same height and colouring.

By four in the morning, Tressy knew that she was not going to find Nora by herself and that she would have to get help, so she turned back towards Cap Martin, taking the road that skirted the private beaches, the gaily-coloured umbrellas and loungers all locked away for the night now. She saw some people on the beach, almost hidden in the dark shadow of a tall stack of wooden loungers, and slowed down, her eyes probing the darkness. Stopping at the kerb, she took off her crash helmet and heard the sound of male laughter, not the amused kind but a lewd, excited laugh. Then she heard a female voice. Without hesitation, she got off the bike and ran down to the group of figures, her feet making no sound on the soft sand.

There were four youths, standing in a small circle, and they were passing a tall, fair-haired girl from hand to hand. Literally from hand to hand, for Nora's dress was pulled down to her waist so that they could fondle her, and one youth put his hand up her skirt. Tressy descended on them like a hell-cat, lashing out at the youths with her crash helmet and screaming at them at the top of her voice. They didn't know what had hit them and didn't stop to find out, taking to their heels and running as Tressy picked up a handful of pebbles and threw them at them, several of the stones finding their mark as the youths yelped in pain and fright as they ran.

But there were four of them and only one of her, so Tressy knew that she'd have to get her cousin away quickly before the youths recovered and came back. But Nora was as drunk as only a girl who isn't used to a lot of strong alcohol can be. She had sunk down on to the ground and was looking vaguely round, her head swaying as if her neck couldn't support it properly. Tressy put her arms into her dress and zipped it up for her, then hauled her to her feet. 'Come on, Nora. I'm going to take you home.'

'Don't wanna go home.'

Nora pulled back, but Tressy hauled her up the beach towards the road. 'Yes, you do. You're very tired and you want to go to bed.'

They reached the scooter and Nora drew back. 'Not going on that. Wanna go in a car.'

'We haven't got a car. You'll have to go on the bike. It'll be all right. Here, put my crash helmet on.'

'No. Don't wanna go,' Nora protested childishly, her face setting into petulant lines.

Tressy was tired and afraid that the youths would come back, and there was no one around now who could help them. 'Nora, will you for God's sake shut up and get on the bike?' she yelled fiercely.

Nora stared at her owlishly for a moment, then she obediently hitched up her skirt and got on the passenger seat. With a sigh of relief, Tressy got on herself. 'Now hold tight,' she commanded. 'We'll soon be home.'

They set off with Tressy steering with one hand whenever it was possible so that she could hold on to Nora's arms round her waist, afraid the other girl might fall off. She turned inland as soon as she could, to get away from the youths, and took the steeply climbing road towards Roquebrune, but she had only gone about half a mile when Nora shouted in her ear. 'Tressy. Tressy, I feel sick!' she wailed.

Cursing, Tressy came to a stop near some trees and helped her cousin behind a bush, where she was horribly sick. Afraid that she might want to be ill again, Tressy sat her down against a tree trunk, but this proved to be a mistake, because Nora just fell asleep. 'Oh, Nora! Come on, wake up.' But even though Tressy shook her exasperatedly, all Nora did was to mumble a protest and didn't even open her eyes. 'Hell. Now what am I going to do?' But Tressy knew that there was no way she was going to get her cousin home on the bike in that state.

Leaving Nora where she was, Tressy found a phone box and for the second time that night rang Michel. To her surprise it was answered almost at once.

'Michel, it's Tressy again. No, I'm not ringing from home, I'm in Monte Carlo. Yes. Yes, it's all right, I've found her.'

'How is she? Is she all right?' Michel demanded anxiously.

'Well, yes, but she seems to have had a lot to drink and she's passed out on me. I can't get her home. Michel, could you . . .?'

'*Mais certainement.*' He agreed instantly. 'Tell me where you are.'

On the Roquebrune road, near the Monte Carlo country club.'

'I know. I will be there in ten minutes.'

'Oh, thank you, But, Michel—you will come alone, won't you? You—you won't bring Cris?'

'Cris is not here. He has gone back to his boat.'

Michel was better than his word, arriving just over five minutes later, a worried frown on his face. He picked Nora up and put her into the car, then said, 'We cannot take her home like that. We will go to my apartment and try to make her more sober.'

Between them they managed to get Nora up to his third floor flat and laid her on the bed. Michel gently tried to wake her while Tressy made black coffee. When she came back from the kitchen Nora was held in Michel's arms and she was sobbing helplessly into his shoulder. But what really made Tressy stare was the fact that Michel was murmuring endearments to her in French, calling her his poor darling and little cabbage, patting her shoulder and kissing her hair. Quickly Tressy set down the coffee and went into Michel's bathroom, amazed at what she had seen. So Michel really cared for Nora! He had always shown a preference for her company, of course, when they had been out as a foursome, but he had never let his feelings show. Probably because Nora had always made it clear that she preferred Cris.

There was an aerosol can of shaving cream on Michel's washbasin; Tressy picked it up and drew a sad clown's face on the mirror, with triangular eyes and woeful, down-turned mouth. Why couldn't love be simple, with people loving those who loved them? But better still, perhaps, not to feel love at all; think what a lot of problems it would solve in the world. Nora wouldn't have slashed her wrist over Cris, and Michel wouldn't have had to stand by and watch the girl he wanted making a fool of herself over someone else. And Cris? And herself? They would never have made love on the beach. She would never have known ... Tressy resolutely thrust the thought aside and looked at her watch. Ten minutes. Nora should have recovered herself a little by now.

She went back into the bedroom where Nora was trying to sip coffee, but she was more than half asleep.

'I think we'd better let her sleep for a couple of hours,' suggested Michel. 'What about her parents?'

'They're in bed. They don't know she's out.'

Michel nodded and laid Nora down on the bed, gently taking off her shoes and pulling the cover over her. His gentleness tore at Tressy's heart and she could hardly swallow the lump that came into her throat.

Michel went to move away, but Nora caught his hand. 'Don't leave me. Please, Michel, don't leave me!'

He looked at Tressy and she nodded. 'Go ahead. I'll sleep on a chair.' At the door she looked back and saw Michel stretch out on the bed beside Nora, on top of the covers, his arms round her comfortingly. She turned off the light and softly closed the door.

At seven-thirty in the morning they sneaked Nora into the villa and she stayed in bed all day, not getting up until dinner. Tressy wasn't so lucky and had to cope with Aunt Grace being unusually demanding. She was at home all day, but Uncle Jack took himself off soon after breakfast carrying his golf clubs, and from the way they snapped at each other, Tressy soon put two and two together and found out that Uncle Jack had been caught paying too much attention to Mrs Young. So, all in all, it wasn't a very happy household, and Aunt Grace, even fatter now from the weeks of rich living, took it out on Tressy by giving her loads of work to do.

Michel came round that evening and Nora greeted him rather shyly at first, having woken up with him lying beside her and not remembering much about how she had got there. He soon put her at ease, though, and now he let his feelings show so that she flushed and began to smile again. Whether she remembered what had happened to her the previous night before Tressy had found her, they didn't know and Nora didn't say. It would be much better if she had forgotten.

For the next few days Michel was a constant visitor, sometimes taking Nora out when she wanted to go, but Nora seemed oddly chastened and was content at the moment with a quiet life, swimming in the pool or going down to the beach to sunbathe with him. Tressy kept out of their way, sometimes taking the scooter into Monte Carlo or one of the other Riviera towns, but finding no enjoyment in being alone. Cris's name was carefully not mentioned by any of them, although Tressy would have given a great deal to find out what had happened between him and Nora. He was constantly in her thoughts and in her dreams and it was hard not to let it show. Every day when she went out she took the road that overlooked the harbour, but his boat had gone and left only an empty space, like a gap in a set of teeth. Well, it was hardly surprising that he had gone, after the way she had turned on him. Rejection was something that most men couldn't take.

Or women, either, if it came to that, Tressy thought, remembering Nora's desperation.

One evening, she came across Michel sitting outside on the terrace alone, waiting for Nora to finish getting ready.

'Hi. Going somewhere interesting?'

'I am taking Nora to have dinner with an aunt of mine who lives in Villefranche.'

Well, that sounded promising. Tressy sat down in the chair opposite him and they were silent for a while as Tressy tried to stop herself asking about Cris. But she just *had* to know. As casually as she could, she said, 'I notice that the *Chimera* is gone from the harbour '

Michel turned to look at her. 'Yes,' he said unhelpfully.

'Has he—moved on?'

'Who?'

'Cris, of course,' she answered tartly.

'Why? Are you interested?'

Tressy frowned. 'Don't play games with me, Michel. If you don't want to tell me or have been told not to, then just say so. But don't play games.'

He looked at her face intently for a moment, then sat back in his chair. 'Cris is still in France but has moved farther along the coast. I do not know whether he will be coming back this summer or not.'

'I see.'

'If you wish I could perhaps contact him for you.'

'No.' She stood up. 'Please don't bother. I'm really not that interested. Excuse me, will you?' And she went inside.

Nora and Michel were quite late coming home that evening and Michel didn't come round until after lunch the next day. In the morning, to Tressy's surprise, Nora came to join her where she was sitting by the pool, mending an evening dress belonging to Aunt Grace that had been torn at the hem.

'Busy?' asked Nora, sitting down beside her.

'Not terribly. Why, what do you want done?'

'What? Oh, nothing. I just wondered—Michel said Cris had left Monte Carlo?'

'So I understand.' Tressy said it steadily, but the needle trembled in her hand. 'What time's Michel coming?' she asked, trying to change the subject.

But Nora wasn't to be sidetracked. 'Did you—like Cris?'

Tressy shrugged and kept her eyes fixed on her work. 'He was okay.'

'Why did he leave?'

At that, Tressy looked up. 'You tell me,' she said sharply. 'You saw him last.'

'But I didn't do or say anything to . . . It was the other way. . . .' Nora stopped, a puzzled frown on her face.

Tressy waited for her to go on, but when she didn't asked, almost reluctantly, 'Just what *did* happen that time you met Cris for lunch?'

But a closed obstinate look that she recognised appeared on Nora's face and she knew even before her cousin spoke that she wasn't going to get anything out of her.

'It's none of your business. I just wondered what made Cris go away, that's all.' And she got up and walked away, which left Tressy wondering just which man her cousin was interested in, and whether she was still hoping that Cris would come back.

When Michel came the two seemed to have a lot to talk about, but Tressy left them to it. She went into Monte Carlo and walked up to the leather shop where she had seen the snakeskin bag. She had looked at it several times since and fallen more in love with it every time. Now, to cheer herself up, she decided on impulse to treat herself and buy it, but to her extreme disappointment the shop was shut. There was a notice on the door saying that the proprietors had gone to a funeral but the shop would be open tomorrow. And tomorrow was the last day of the sale. Tressy could imagine the bag being beyond her reach again just as she had made up her mind to buy it, and determined to come again in the morning to make sure she got it.

That evening, Michel surprised her by asking her to go out with them on his yacht the next day.

'But surely you don't want me along?' she demurred, not even sure that she wanted to go and play gooseberry all day anyway.

'But we insist. Nora feels a little nervous about sailing boats, and it would be good if you came, too.'

To act as nursemaid to Nora and to crew the boat, Tressy thought wryly. Still, it would be better than staying home alone. She nodded. 'Okay, I'll come along. But I have to go into Monte Carlo first to get something.'

'*Bien*. I will bring the boat round to the harbour and meet you both there at ten-thirty. That will give you enough time, *n'est-ce pas*?'

Tressy assured him that it would, and rather wondered what she'd let herself in for. But she arrived at the harbour the next morning in good time, dressed in shorts and a top over a bikini, and carrying the precious handbag, carefully packed into a box. She saw Nora waving to her and walked along the quay to have a look at Michel's boat. It was larger than she had expected, about twenty feet long, and had beautifully graceful lines. It was comparatively new and looked as if Michel lavished a great deal of care on it, the deck well varnished and clean and all the chrome and brass sparkling in the sun.

'Come and look in the cabin,' enthused Nora. 'It's really neat.'

Tressy went aboard and was genuinely surprised. 'It's a beautiful boat,' she complimented Michel. 'Why didn't you take us out on it before...' She broke off, not knowing how to finish.

'I lent it to a friend for his honeymoon,' he told them with a smile. 'It makes a good boat for a honeymoon, *non*? As long as you do not rock it too much.'

As the girls laughed at him the boat tilted as someone else came on board.

'Anyone at home?'

Tressy stood very still as she heard Cris's voice. Then she looked quickly at Nora and Michel and found them watching her, quite unsurprised. So they'd planned this. Stiffly she said to Michel, 'Is there somewhere safe I could put my parcel?'

'Of course. In this drawer,' He pulled it open for her and then went on deck to greet Cris.

Tressy looked at Nora and saw that she was a little pale under her tan. Maybe she had reasons for not wanting to see Cris again as well. But she turned and went on deck ahead of Tressy.

'Hallo, Crispin, how are you?'

'Fine. And you're looking very well, Nora.'

For once she didn't object to him shortening her name, and merely nodded and went to help Michel cast off.

Cris turned as she came slowly out of the cabin and said evenly, 'Hallo, Tressy.' He was dressed in the usual holiday wear of shorts and cotton T-shirt, but he didn't look in a holiday mood, his lips were set into a grim line and there was a guarded look in his eyes.

Tressy wanted to go to him, to reach out and touch him, but her courage failed her and she answered

woodenly, 'Hallo, Crispin,' and went to find herself a
place on the foredeck out of the reach of those dark eyes.

It felt strange and yet somehow familiar for them to
be out in a foursome again. But now everything had
changed and the tension between Tressy and Cris
crackled like volatile electricity. She caught him
looking at her and flushed deeply, knowing that he
was remembering that tempestuous hour on the beach
when they had lain naked in each other's arms, lost to
everything but the gratification of their sexual hunger.
She had been exposed, then, to his eyes, to his mouth
and hands. A shudder ran through her and she turned
quickly away to hide it, wishing that the day would
end, unable to stand the torture of seeing him.

They sailed down the coast to Italy and anchored in
a cove for lunch, ferrying the food across to the beach
in the little dinghy they towed behind them. Tressy
tried not to be left alone with Cris and hung on to
Nora like a leech, but the others seemed determined to
leave them together. When they had eaten Michel
suggested a stroll along the beach, and Nora got up to
join him. Tressy rose, too, but Cris caught her wrist.
'No. Stay here. It's about time we talked,' he added as
the others moved away.

Tressy disengaged her wrist and shrugged. 'What is
there to talk about?' Kneeling down on the sand, she
began to pack up the remains of the picnic.

'The last time we met, for a start,' Cris said grimly.

'Oh, that.'

'Yes, *that*.' Then, exasperatedly. 'Will you please
leave those things alone and look at me?'

'All right, if that's what you want.' She sat on the
sand and looked up at him where he stood tall against
the sun. Her heart skipped a couple of beats, but she
made herself say calmly, 'I really don't see that there's
anything to discuss.'

Cris's mouth tightened. 'I was concerned about you.'

'Why?' Tressy dug her hands into the sand so that he couldn't see them trembling. 'It wasn't any big deal,' she added deliberately.

There was a long moment of shattering silence before Cris said stiffly, 'So it didn't mean anything to you?'

'Why should it?' Tressy asked him coldly.

'I thought it was something more than just a casual lay,' Cris replied bitingly. 'Evidently I was wrong.'

'That's right. It meant as little to me as it did to you.' Getting to her feet, Tressy began to carry the picnic things over to the dinghy. Cris followed her.

'And I trust there won't be any—shall we say unfortunate outcome to that night?'

Tressy swung round to look at him, her face cold and set. 'You don't have to worry, you won't get any paternity suits thrown at you; I know how to take care of myself.'

Cris's eyes ran over her disparagingly. 'I felt sure you would,' he told her, making it sound like an insult, then turned and strode away down the beach, leaving Tressy hating him, herself and just being alive.

They didn't speak to each other again, making Nora and Michel look at each other ruefully when they returned and realised the situation. Michel suggested they cut short the trip and return to Menton, where he usually kept his boat, and then take a taxi on to Monte Carlo, and everyone agreed. There was enough breeze to fill the sails and they made good time on the way back. Ordinarily Tressy would have loved the way the boat moved with the wind, but she felt so wretched that all she wanted to do was to get the whole thing over. Tomorrow, she decided, no matter what Uncle Jack said, she was going home; she just couldn't take any more of this. She sat on the foredeck, Cris staying in the cockpit with the others, and he didn't come for'ard until they neared Menton harbour and he came to let down the sails so that they could go in on the engine.

It was a lovely, peaceful day with lots of small boats and windsurfers on the water, the beaches crowded with sunbathers, a perfect summer day to be on holiday. When Cris came for'ard, Tressy moved her legs out of the way and looked up, unable to keep her eyes off him. Cris's glance met hers and he opened his mouth to speak, but whatever he was going to say was lost beneath the explosion of sound and flame that ripped through the boat as Michel turned on the engine.

Cris staggered as the boat rolled under the impact and almost fell into the sea, but managed to grab the sail and hang on. Tressy was thrown to one side but immediately scrambled to her feet. She screamed out, 'Nora!' and tried to get through the flames coming out of the cabin windows to the back of the boat, but Cris came after her and pulled her back.

'Nora's all right—Michel will take care of her. Come on, jump!'

But Tressy tried to fight him off and get to the cabin. 'My new handbag's in there!'

'Forget it. For God's sake, jump!' Acrid black smoke was blowing towards them and the flames had started to run up the rigging.

'Are you crazy? That bag cost me six hundred francs!'

With a furious oath, Cris picked her up bodily and threw her over the side, then he jumped in himself as another explosion ripped through the yacht.

'Swim away from it!' he yelled at her, and came to put his hand on her shoulder to make sure she obeyed him.

They swam a good twenty yards away and then Tressy trod water, looking round for her cousin. Nora and Michel were both in the sea and Tressy waved to her, but Michel was hanging on to the dinghy, trying to untie it and tow it away before it, too, caught fire.

Cris said, 'I'll go and help him. Will you be all right?'

'Yes. Be be careful.'

He looked at her for a second, then broke into a fast crawl and swam away.

Behind her there was the shriek of a siren as an orange and blue rescue boat came surging out of the harbour towards them. The harbour wall, all the way up to the lighthouse, was lined with people, avidly watching. Tressy turned away and saw that the whole of the yacht was now in flames, the great pall of smoke rising high into the sullied blue of the sky. They had managed to untie the dinghy and pull it clear of the flames before the rescue boat came surging up. It picked up the others and took the dinghy in tow before turning to come for her. They left the yacht where it was to burn itself out.

Neither Nora nor Michel were hurt at all except that Michel's eyebrows were a bit singed, and Nora seemed to be all right on the rescue boat, but when they got ashore shock hit her and she started to get hysterical. Tressy moved to look after her, but Michel firmly took over, giving Nora a shake and then holding her in his arms to let her cry it out on his shoulder. Somebody rushed up with a blanket to put round Nora's shoulders and someone else gave her a glass of cognac. Cris was busy with the officials, giving names and addresses. Tressy watched rather helplessly, then turned and slipped through the crowd and climbed the steps from the quay to the top of the wall. She sat on the edge and watched the fire gradually diminish as the flames ate away everything there was to burn. Then the rescue boat went out again and pulled in what was left of the hull, the vile smell of burnt fibreglass filling the nostrils of the large crowd that had gathered to watch.

A taxi drove up and Michel put Nora into it, had a few minutes of rapid conversation with Cris, then got into it himself and it drove away. Cris started to look round the crowd, for Tressy presumably, but then the harbourmaster claimed his attention again. The crowd of people began to drift back to the town and beaches when they realised that they had seen all there was to see and the burnt out boat was left, just about floating sluggishly in the water. Slowly Tressy got up and went down to look at it more closely.

Black smuts blew off it on to her legs and the smell made her feel sick, but she peered at what was once the cabin area, then picked up a piece of stick and poked about in the debris where the drawers had been. After a couple of minutes she unearthed a tarnished frame and length of what had once been gold chain, all that was left of her lovely handbag. Carefully she hooked up the chain and caught it in her hand.

'A souvenir?' Cris's sarcastic voice asked as she stood looking down at it.

Raising her head, she met his gaze steadily enough. 'Something like that.'

'We can go now. I've taken care of all the arrangements about the boat.'

'What will happen to it?'

'A crane will lift it out of the water on to the quay until the insurance people come down to have a look at it. Then I expect it will be scrapped.'

He turned to walk down the quay, but Tressy took a last look at the boat. 'Why did it catch fire?' she asked.

'We think there must have been a gas leak which

built up in the hull, then, when Michel turned on the engine, a spark ignited the gas and it blew up.' He waited a moment. 'Are you coming?'

'What? Oh, yes.' Tressy turned to walk with him, but put up a hand to hide her face.

'We'll get a taxi and I'll drop you off at the villa and . . .' He stopped, then caught her hand and pulled it down. 'You're crying!' he exclaimed in disbelief.

'So what? Leave me alone.' Hastily she rubbed at her eyes with her free hand.

'Why? Because your handbag got burnt?' Cris asked sardonically. 'What was in it that was so precious— your book of telephone numbers? Or was it just money that you wanted to risk your life to save?'

'Shut up! Damn you, shut up. Oh God, it was such a beautiful boat!' And suddenly the tears were pouring down her cheeks in an unstoppable flood.

'Tressy.' Cris said her name on a guarded note of wonder. He lifted his arms as if to put them round her, but hesitated in case she fought him off again.

But Tressy looked at him imploringly and said, 'Hold me. Please hold me.'

So he put his arm round her and held her very close, his hand stroking her hair, much to the interest of passers-by. After a few minutes Tressy muttered something against his shoulder and he loosened his hold so that he could see her face. She sniffed and tried to wipe her eyes with her hands. 'Oh hell! In front of all these people, too. And I swore I wouldn't.'

Cris put up a finger to wipe a last tear from her cheek. 'It's best to let it go. I thought you were upset because you'd lost your bag.'

'Well, maybe it was for that, too,' Tressy admitted honestly. 'It was a brand new one; I only bought it this morning. It cost six hundred francs. That probably doesn't mean much to you, but it's more than I've ever spent on myself in my life. It took me a long time to make up my mind to spend that much money. But I was so miserable that I . . .' She broke off, her face flushing.

'Why were you so miserable?' Cris turned her towards him, looking searchingly into her face. 'Tell me,' he insisted.

Tressy hesitated for a moment, but instinct told her that she couldn't draw back now, so she straightened up and asked, 'Why did you take Nora out the day after we—we were together?'

'So that's it!' Cris gazed at her with relieved amusement mixed up with annoyance. 'So Nora didn't tell you? Still, I suppose that's understandable. But why you should think that I wanted Nora after what we'd had together . . .' He gave an exasperated laugh. 'I took Nora out to lunch so that I could tell her in plain words that I wasn't interested in her and never had been.'

Her face white, Tressy exclaimed, 'Oh, you should never have done that!'

'Why not?—it's true. And I thought it about time she faced up to it.'

'But she might have tried to . . .' she hesitated, then finished slowly, 'to kill herself again.'

Cris stared at her, appalled. 'You'd better tell me,' he ordered grimly.

So, standing there on the quay, with people walking past, and the stone houses of the old town rising to the cathedral behind them, Tressy told him why she had broken their date and tried to avoid him.

Cris groaned. 'Nora really messed things up between us, didn't she? I had no idea she felt that deeply, but I must admit that I wasn't paying her a great deal of attention, my thoughts were entirely elsewhere. But why didn't you tell me? We could have worked something out.'

Looking down at her feet, Tressy said, 'Do you think we could find that taxi now? I haven't got any shoes and these stones are hurting my feet.'

'We'll find somewhere more comfortable by all means, but you needn't think you're going to evade the issue that easily. You still have quite a lot of explaining to do, young lady.'

They found an outdoor café under the arches of the promenade and Cris insisted they sit together on one of the double seats almost surrounded by tall plants in wooden tubs that gave them privacy from the other customers. Tressy rubbed the soles of her feet. 'You were lucky,' she said, envious of his rope-soled deck shoes.

'Doubly lucky; my wallet was in the pocket of my shorts, so I'll be able to pay for some drinks.' He produced a still wet note for the waiter and then, in a tone that wasn't to be denied, said, 'Now tell me.'

Tressy sighed. 'I didn't tell you about Nora because—well, because I thought she was so much in love with you that she had the right to try and attract you, or however you care to put it, without me getting in the way.'

'And didn't you think that you also had the right?'

Tressy stirred her coffee and shook her head.

'Why not?'

'Because—because I wasn't sure that I—how I . . . Oh, dear! I just wasn't sure how I felt about you, that's all.'

'I see.' Cris put a hand on her neck under the thick red fall of her hair and Tressy lifted up her head to gaze at him, her lips parting sensuously. 'But it seems that you did make up your mind about me later. Only I still don't know which way.' He gave a crooked, self-mocking grin. 'When we made love I thought you meant it. But then you turned round and told me you hated me—which was quite a smack in the face for a man in those circumstances. So which was right, Tressy? Love or hate?'

'Both.' Leaning back against the cushions, she gazed into his face, lifting a finger to trace his profile. 'I loved what we did together, but afterwards, when I came back to my senses, I realised what Nora might do if you—claimed me, and I hated you for putting me into that position, and myself for letting you, I suppose.'

'Idiot,' Cris put a hand on her waist and drew her closer. 'Do you still hate me?'

'No,' she admitted on little more than a whisper.

'Good. I was afraid Nora was coming between us, that's why I told her I wasn't interested. I could also have told her that I was head over heels in love with you, but I wanted to tell you that myself. Only you wouldn't give me a chance.'

'How could I, when you went away?' Tressy objected indignantly. 'Your boat was gone when I looked in the harbour.'

'So you did care a little!' Cris exclaimed triumphantly. 'I thought I'd clear out to let Michel have a chance with Nora, but I gave him strict instructions to get in touch if you asked about me. And a couple of days ago you did, so we fixed up the trip today between us. Although that, too, didn't work out as I'd hoped.'

'You mean the boat blowing up?'

'No, I mean the row we had at lunchtime. And you know it.'

'Mm. We always seem to end up quarrelling.'

'Not always. I can think of one notable exception,' he told her meaningfully.

Tressy flushed a little and smiled. Cris was sitting very close, their faces only a few inches apart, and she wondered why he didn't kiss her, but then the reason came to her and she leaned forward and kissed him lingeringly on the mouth. 'I love you,' she said softly. 'I'll always love you.'

He gave a long sigh. 'Well, it's about time.' And he pulled her close into his arms to kiss her with the fierce joy of possession.

It was early evening before they left the café and walked up into the town to find a taxi. Tressy had Cris's shirt over her bikini, but she derived more warmth from his closeness and the arm he put across her shoulders.

In the taxi, he started to make plans. 'I'll come to the villa with you to make sure that Nora is all right, then go on down to the boat to change. What time shall I call for you? We must go somewhere really special tonight to celebrate. And you must tell your uncle so that we can go back to England soon and I can meet your mother.'

'My mother?' Tressy looked at him in astonishment. 'Why do you want to meet my mother?'

'Well, it is customary for a man to meet his girl's people before they get married, you know.'

Tressy sat up straight and stared at him. 'Married?'

Cris looked amused. 'Did I forget to mention that? Sorry.'

'Yes, I rather think you did forget it,' Tressy said hollowly.

'Then I'd better remedy that at once.' Taking hold of her hands, Cris said softly, 'Will you marry me, Tressy?' and confidently waited for her answer.

She gazed into his face and knew that she would never love anyone else, but she disengaged her hands and shook her head. 'No, Cris, I won't marry you. I'm sorry.'

He stared at her, completely stunned. 'You can't mean it?'

'Yes, I do. I don't want to get married.'

The taxi jolted before he could say anything else and she saw that they had arrived at the villa.

'Wait,' Cris ordered the driver as he got out. Then he took Tressy firmly by the arm and led her into the garden. 'You said you loved me,' he accused.

'And I do. I'll come back to the boat with you now if you like so that we can be together. And I'll stay with you for as long as you want. But can't you see? I don't want to be—to be owned.'

'No, I don't see,' Cris answered shortly. 'You either love someone enough to marry them or you don't.'

'But the world isn't like that any more,' Tressy protested. 'You can commit yourself to someone without having to go through the mumbo-jumbo of a ceremony to prove it.'

'Then maybe I'm the old-fashioned type. I love you and I want to marry you.'

'You don't have to make an honest woman of me, if that's what you're thinking,' Tressy retorted sharply, anger beginning to grow.

'It wasn't. But maybe you think if we're not married you'll still be able to sleep around.'

She lifted a hand to hit him, but he caught her wrist. 'Maybe I slept around once too often,' she said fiercely. 'With you!'

His grip tightened. 'And perhaps I don't like the idea of being good enough to go to bed with but not good enough to marry.'

'I told you; I don't want to be owned. I want to be independent and earn my own living. You have too much. I don't want to have to be grateful for the food I eat, the clothes I wear or the roof over my head. Now do you understand?'

'Oh, sure, I understand.' He let go of her wrist in

disgust. 'There's no need for any gratitude in marriage. You're just a snob.'

'A snob?' Tressy stared at him incredulously. 'How can I be a snob? I'm not rich.'

'You don't have to be. There's such a thing as inverse snobbery, where the poor look down on those better off and take pride in being poor. Well, okay, if that's what you want, then go ahead and live with your pride. But I want a loving wife, not someone who'll come to my bed when she has time in between running her own selfish life!' Then he turned sharply on his heel and began to stride away.

'Where are you going?' demanded Tressy.

'Back to my boat. And I shall be there for a few days if you change your mind. If not, then goodbye, it's been nice knowing you.' He walked on as she gazed after him. 'Tell Nora I asked after her.' And then he was out of sight.

Tressy stood there, sure he would come back, but she heard the taxi start up and began to run, but it had gone before she reached the driveway.

Slowly she turned and went into the house, expecting to find Nora in bed, recovering from her ordeal by fire and water, but to her surprise they were all in the drawing-room with glasses of champagne in their hands.

'Come on, Tressy. Come on in, girl,' Uncle Jack called out as she hesitated in the doorway. 'We've some good news to celebrate. Here, have a glass of champagne. Nora's just told us that she and Michel are getting married.'

Almost in a trance, Tressy took the glass and raised it in a toast. Nora looked almost beautiful, her make-up washed off and her eyes sparkling happily in her tanned face, and Michel, too, looked very happy. He might have caught Nora on the rebound and be very glad of the money she stood to inherit, but Tressy believed he really cared about her cousin and she was happy to wish them well. They were all going out to celebrate and they invited Tressy along, so she went because it was better than staying home alone and she wouldn't have time to think.

She put on the dress that Cris had bought her, put her hair up into a sophisticated style and was careful over her make-up. Michel had booked a table at the casino restaurant and afterwards they watched the elaborate and fabulous floor show. A great many men looked her over that night and liked what they saw, but Tressy was quite unaware of it. She was like two people, one who was outwardly normal, talking and smiling, and the other completely numb, unable and unwilling to think or feel. Luckily Michel and Nora were too wrapped up in each other tonight to ask her questions about Cris, but she knew that sooner or later they would get curious.

It was almost two in the morning when she left the Casino with Aunt Grace and Uncle Jack, leaving the engaged couple to dance the night away. She said good night quite naturally and went up to her room, but once there she just lay on the bed without undressing and stared at the ceiling. Now she could think, now she could feel. And she didn't enjoy either.

At three, she suddenly stood up, grabbed a few things that she stuffed into a holdall, wrote a quick note that she propped up on her dressing-table, then crept silently out of the house. The breeze lifted her skirts as she drove the scooter down into Monte Carlo, attracting a few wolf whistles. She wished the machine was more powerful, it seemed to take forever before she got to the harbour and drove along the quay, pulling up just by the *Chimera*. The gangplank was down and she went across it unsteadily in the dark and her high heels. Dropping her bag in the cockpit, she went down to the cabins. Cris's door wasn't locked. She pushed it open and saw him lying in a shaft of moonlight. He was awake, lying with his hands under his head, only a thin sheet covering him.

Tressy moved into the cabin and shut the door, then began to take off her clothes as he watched. 'Is there room for someone else in there?' she asked him as her dress fell to the floor.

'There could be,' he answered, watching the play of moonlight on her slender body. 'But only for a wife.'

Moving over to the bed, Tressy pulled back the sheet. He wasn't wearing anything. 'Will a fiancée do for now?' she suggested huskily.

'A fiancée will do fine.' Moving over, he put his arms round her as she climbed in beside him. 'What took you so long?' he demanded as he gathered her to him. 'I thought you weren't coming.'

'But I'm here. And I'm never going away again, my love. My husband.'

Here's how to get this special offer from Harlequin!

AUGUST
TREASURY EDITION
COUPON

As simple as 1...2...3!

1. Each month, save one Treasury Edition coupon from your favorite Romance or Presents novel.
2. In four months you'll have saved four Treasury Edition coupons (<u>only one coupon per month allowed</u>).
3. Then all you have to do is fill out and return the order form provided, along with the four Treasury Edition coupons required and $1.00 for postage and handling.

Mail to: Harlequin Reader Service

In the U.S.A.
P.O. Box 52040
Phoenix, AZ 85072-2040

In Canada
P.O. Box 2800, Postal Station A
5170 Yonge Street
Willowdale, Ont. M2N 6J3

RT1-A-2

Please send me my FREE copy of the Janet Dailey Treasury Edition. I have enclosed the four Treasury Edition coupons required and $1.00 for postage and handling along with this order form.

(Please Print)

NAME_____

ADDRESS_____

CITY_____

STATE/PROV._____ ZIP/POSTAL CODE_____

SIGNATURE_____
This offer is limited to one order per household.

SUPPLIES LIMITED

This special Janet Dailey offer expires January 1986.

You're invited to accept
4 books and a
surprise gift Free!

Acceptance Card

Mail to: Harlequin Reader Service®

In the U.S.
2504 West Southern Ave.
Tempe, AZ 85282

In Canada
P.O. Box 2800, Postal Station A
5170 Yonge Street
Willowdale, Ontario M2N 6J3

YES! Please send me 4 free Harlequin Presents® novels and my free surprise gift. Then send me 8 brand new novels every month as they come off the presses. Bill me at the low price of $1.75 each ($1.95 in Canada)—an 11% saving off the retail price. There are no shipping, handling or other hidden costs. There is no minimum number of books I must purchase. I can always return a shipment and cancel at any time. Even if I never buy another book from Harlequin, the 4 free novels and the surprise gift are mine to keep forever.

108 BPP-BPGE

Name _____ (PLEASE PRINT) _____

Address _____ Apt. No. _____

City _____ State/Prov. _____ Zip/Postal Code _____

This offer is limited to one order per household and not valid to present subscribers. Price is subject to change.

ACP-SUB-1